WOLF CLAIMED

SUPERNATURAL SANCTUARY BOOK 1

KELLIE MCALLEN

COVER DESIGN BY
Covers by Christian

CHAPTER 1

LUNA

You know how animals can sense when a storm is brewing? They get restless and agitated like they know something is about to happen, but they don't know what, or when, and there's nothing they can do to prepare for it. Well, that's exactly how I felt the day the shit storm hit, and my world came crashing down around me.

When my alarm rang, I woke from a restless doze, tossed off my thin, fleece blanket and kicked myself free of the sheet that was pasted to my legs with sweat. I clawed away the strands of tangled, dark hair that clung to my damp neck. My body always tended to run kind of hot, but that day I felt like a tamale being steamed inside a corn husk. My normally smooth sheets and soft, fuzzy blanket were about as comfortable as sandpaper.

I didn't feel sick exactly, although my body seemed achy and feverish. I felt a little nauseous, but my belly was growling like my stomach was a rabid dog, eating me alive. I didn't need to throw up, I needed to eat.

But the bowl of Lucky Charms I usually ate for breakfast didn't sound the least bit appealing. I wanted meat. Kind of strange for a vegetarian. But maybe not for a half-hearted one like me who thought it was the right thing to do but couldn't seem to remember why when the scent of bacon wafted from the kitchen like it was doing just then.

I tromped down the hall, my body twitchy, my muscles tense like coiled springs, quivering with pent up energy, ready to burst out of my skin. My fingers clenched with the bizarre urge to claw away my flesh. Sounds crazy now that I try to explain it, but at the time I didn't think that much of it. I had no way of knowing what it all meant.

I chalked it up to PMS, especially considering how downright ferocious I felt, like I wanted to rip somebody's head off for no good reason. Zander made a good target, since, as his older sister, it was my duty to keep the cocky, little brat in his place.

"You're in my way." I jabbed an elbow into his ribs, shoving him away from the stove where Mom was frying bacon and eggs like the perfectly happy homemaker she was.

Zander jerked aside, and I took his place, snagging a strip of bacon from the frying pan. He shoved me back with a scowl and tried to yank the bacon from my fingers, but I held on tight, even though the sizzling meat was burning my skin.

"Hey, that's mine! You don't even eat bacon!"

"Today I do. I'm starving. And you've probably already had a dozen pieces."

"So? Mom was making that for me. Cook your own if you want some. Oh wait, I forgot, you can't, because you're a pathetic excuse for a girl." He rolled his eyes and stuck out his tongue like he was five instead of fifteen.

I made an equally juvenile face. "I burnt it one time. You've never even tried to make it."

"Cuz I'm not a girl."

"Oh really? Then why is your voice higher than mine?"

Mom gave that worried little frown she always made when I fought with my brother then reached for the package of bacon. "Don't fight, Luna. It's not ladylike. I can have some more ready in a jif. Or maybe you'd like to try to make it?"

I grimaced and shook my head. Learning how to cook was the last thing I cared about right then. Or any time, really. "I'm too hungry right now. I'd rather eat it raw than wait for it."

Mom nodded with a concerned look on her face then plated the rest of the cooked bacon and handed it to me. "Okay. Eat this and I'll cook some more for Zander."

I felt bad for a millisecond, but I knew she didn't mind. I didn't know how she could stand it, doing nothing but cooking and cleaning all day, tending to her family, especially my father, like he was the center of the universe. But she loved it. I didn't know what I wanted to do when I got out of school, but it certainly wasn't that. I wanted my own identity.

You'd think in this day and age that my parents would be all for that, but no, they both talked like I'd be just like my mom someday. While other parents were encouraging their daughters to go into science, technology, or medicine, mine thought being a wife and mother was the greatest thing a girl could aspire to. I hadn't pushed the issue much yet, but I fully intended to make something of myself before I even thought about settling down. But none of us could imagine what fate had in store for me.

I held the plate to my chin and scarfed down several pieces of bacon, ripping off large chunks and gnawing it violently, before the roaring in my stomach settled a little. No one seemed to notice my unusual behavior, but that was normal. My brother and I were too close in age for me to remember those few years before he was born and they started fussing over him like he was the chosen one.

My body still craved something, but my bacon was gone, and I didn't want any of the eggs, so I stalked off to get ready for school. A lukewarm shower did little to cool my blazing skin. I was tempted to put on shorts, but the icy drizzle pattering against my bedroom window discouraged me. I tugged on some jeans instead. As a concession, I put on a thin tank top then tossed a gauzy shirt over it, letting it hang open, unbuttoned.

I wasn't the type to fuss over my looks like some girls, but something motivated me to swipe on some wine-colored lipstick and brush out my long hair instead of wrapping it up in a topknot to get it off my neck like I usually did. I took a glance in the mirror then sneered at myself, wondering why I cared. It wasn't like I wanted to impress any of the guys at my school. None of them were interesting enough to tempt me into turning into my mother. Well, except maybe one, but he was off limits.

When I was ready, I pounded on Zander's door, yelling, "I'm leaving."

We both knew I wouldn't leave without him and risk getting in trouble, but Zander hustled out anyway, well aware that I'd make him regret it if he kept me waiting. I climbed into my ride—Dad's old, gray pickup that I'd happily claimed when he got a new one because I liked how high up I sat in it. I still felt irritable, so I pulled up my Avril Lavigne playlist, plugged my phone into the aux jack, and cranked up the volume. Zander cringed and reached for the knob, but I batted his hand away.

"What's wrong with you? You're bitchier than normal today."

I scowled at him but answered, glad to have somebody to complain to. "I don't know. I just feel… fierce."

He curled his upper lip that was shadowed with dark peach fuzz about as long as his buzzed-off hair. "That time of the month?"

I punched his shoulder. "Shut up, jerk face."

He winced but resisted the urge to rub the spot even though I knew I'd hit him hard enough to leave a bruise. "You smell weird, too."

I blew that off as a random insult, but when he looked away, I took a quick sniff of my armpit just to be sure. All I could smell was my vanilla-scented body wash.

Once we got to school, Zander covered his head with his jacket and darted towards the building, but I stalked defiantly across the parking lot, face to the sky, savoring the cold water that pelted my flushed skin. Once inside, I tipped my head back and whipped my hair back and forth, shaking the water from my mane like a dog. The move drew the attention of several people, including Nikko Brisbane and his gang.

I didn't know then what they were, but maybe my subconscious recognized them instinctually. They reminded me of wild animals, the way they slunk around the school, their dark eyes leering like they were hunting for prey. They were always in a group, with Nikko at the center, communicating with each other with wordless looks and nods, giving off a menacing vibe that warned me to stay away.

My father had given me the same warning on several occasions when we saw any of them around town. His reaction alone would've been enough, the way he bristled and stiffened when he saw them, like they were hardened criminals instead of teenage boys. But he always made a point to say something, too, reminding me to stay away from "those boys from the other side of the river." I thought it had more to do with his family than Nikko himself, because I remember my dad having an even worse reaction to Nikko's father once.

They'd come face to face over an animal trap in the hunting supply store when I was ten. Dad's whole body had swelled up and hardened like he was about to turn into the Incredible Hulk. His eyes bulged with a ferocious look, and he bared his teeth before shoving me behind him. Nikko's father acted the same way, and they both slowly backed away from each other. We left the store without buying what we came for, then Dad hustled me into his truck and peeled out like the building was about to explode. For the next several months, he drove twenty minutes to the next town over whenever he wanted something.

When I got my license, it took months to convince my dad to let me go to town on my own. Once I did, he would question me every time I went out about where I'd been and who I was with. He never said what he was so worried about, but I had a feeling he thought that Nikko and his friends would get to me.

I didn't understand what my father had against them. While they definitely gave off scary vibes, as far as I knew they'd never done anything to warrant that kind of distrust. But he never gave me an explanation, and my father wasn't the kind of man you questioned. His word was law, and all he needed was a stone-faced look to enforce it.

But I was as hard-headed as my father, and there was something about Nikko that drew me in. With dark hair, tan skin, and piercing, amber eyes, Nikko caught the attention of most girls in school. But it was the dangerous energy he radiated that attracted me even though it should have repelled. It was only the fact that Nikko treated me with the same aversion my father had for him that kept me away from him. Until then.

When Nikko's gaze landed on me, tossing my hair, his nostrils flared, and his mouth stretched open with a hiss like he was tasting the air. His followers did the same thing. Nikko's eyes zeroed in on me, roving slowly up and down my body before boring into mine with an intensity that made me shiver. Fear and attraction coursed through me at the same time, like competing bolts of electricity zigzagging through me that crackled and sparked as they collided, raising my hackles and my libido at the same time.

"Luna," Zander whispered tersely. Dad's admonitions were not restricted to me. Zander had been warned against Nikko and his group, too.

From the corner of my eye, I could see my brother tense and flick his eyes back and forth between us as Nikko took a step closer. I sucked in a deep breath as he neared, drawing in a musky scent too intense to be his natural aroma but better than any cologne I'd ever smelled. I desperately wanted to take another sniff, but I was too overwhelmed to breathe. I'd never been that close to him before. He'd always stayed clear of me, like his father had given him the same warning about me as mine had about him.

But for some reason, today was different.

I dared to take another breath as Nikko stepped in front of me and his pack encircled us, fencing me in.

CHAPTER 2

NIKKO

It had been drilled into me my whole life—stay away from the Ammon pack. So why was my body moving towards Luna like a scrap of metal being pulled in by a powerful magnet?

And why were my pack mates following behind me like they had no more control of themselves than I did? I wasn't alpha yet; they didn't have to obey me, even though they'd been practicing for it my whole life. They stayed back some, out of deference to me, but I could tell they were as drawn to her as I was.

It was her scent that drew me towards her, and probably them, too. One whiff of it curled through my body like poison gas, intoxicating me. I'd never smelled anything quite like it. She smelled like a wolf.

Which was no surprise considering who her family was. As much as I avoided any contact with them, I knew exactly what they smelled like. I'd been trained to sniff out the slightest hint of the enemy pack.

But it wasn't the lingering scent of them I smelled on

her. She smelled like a different wolf, altogether. She couldn't be, of course. There were no female wolves, hadn't been for generations.

Had she been hanging out with some other wolf who didn't belong to either of our packs? Doubtful. Pacts stuck to their own territory. Even if they weren't enemies with other packs, they didn't mingle. But even if she had been with another wolf, that wouldn't explain the irresistible pull I felt towards her all of a sudden.

My body moved closer, her scent reeling me in, till I was close enough to touch her. I'd never gotten that close to her before, never been near enough to see the gray flecks in her blue eyes or the pink flush on the porcelain skin that stood out against her damp, dark hair. Striking. I'd always thought she was pretty, but I'd never been so attracted to her.

Desire coursed through my veins like acid, burning me alive. She was the only thing that would quench the fire. I had to have her. My hand lifted to stroke her cheek, but I forced it down. She wouldn't want me to touch her, and I didn't want to scare her away.

Her chest heaved as she took in deep, rapid breaths, tempting me to look at her breasts that were pushing against her tight tank top. I focused my gaze on her beautiful eyes instead, which widened in fear. No doubt, she'd been warned to stay away from me and my pack, though whatever reason she'd been given wasn't the real one. Women weren't privy to the truth about werewolves, not even if they were an alpha's daughter, like Luna.

I stood there, staring at her for a long moment, not sure what to say to her. There was nothing to say. I couldn't very well ask her why she smelled like a wolf or tell her that I had a sudden, irresistible desire to touch her, kiss her, claim her. She'd think I was crazy.

Her breath hitched, and her heart sped up, both signs of fear, but there was another emotion on her face. One that could cause the same reaction. I knew because I felt its effects on my own body. Was she as attracted to me as I was to her?

"Hey Luna. You look really nice today." The words tumbled out of my mouth, and I instantly regretted them. I sounded like a tongue-tied idiot.

She stared back at me for a moment, dumbstruck, but then her wine-stained lips curled up in a smile that sent bolts of pleasure shooting through my body. Oh yeah, she definitely wanted me, too.

"Thank you," she whispered, and the husky sound of her voice vibrated through me.

I didn't know what to say next, but it didn't matter, because her brother worked up the nerve to approach us then—confronting five enemy wolves in an attempt to protect his sister. Pretty impressive for a pup who'd probably turned for the first time less than a year ago. But, like me, Zander was in line to be the next alpha of his pack, so he didn't dare show any weakness.

"Luna, you should get to class," he said, but he kept his eyes on me, staring me down without flinching, only the smallest quiver bristling the hair on his neck.

She frowned at him and opened her mouth to argue, but then the first bell rang. "So should you," she said to him, then slipped between the wolves that surrounded her and walked off.

"Stay away from my sister," Zander growled when she

was out of earshot then backed away a few steps before turning and hurrying off.

"What the heck was that?" Roane, my best friend and most likely my future beta glanced back and forth between Luna and me, his bushy, bronze eyebrows yanked up to his hairline and his big mouth gaping open.

I stared after her, too, till she moved out of sight, then turned my attention to Roane. "Did you… smell her?"

I couldn't imagine that he hadn't, her scent was so potent, but now that she was gone, the whole situation seemed unbelievable. I'd never been attracted to a girl because of how she smelled before, and I'd never been *that* attracted to anyone.

When I glanced at the others, they all nodded with guilty looks on their faces like they felt bad for being attracted to her too, but Roane never bothered to hide his feelings.

"Heck yeah. Damn, she smelled good. Better than bacon and waffles. If I didn't already have a girlfriend, I'd be all over that."

I growled at him, and he held up his hands. "I think she was into you. Are you going to go for it?"

I made a face then stalked out of the lobby and down the hallway, my heavy boots pounding on the tile floors. The crowd parted around us when they saw me coming, giving my group a wide berth. "What? No. Of course not."

"Why not?" Roane scurried to keep up with me, and the rest of my pack mates followed behind us. When I got to my first period class, the others wandered off to their own, but Roane had the same class as me, so he followed me in.

I took my usual seat in the back corner of the classroom, and Roane slid in next to me. The seats around us stayed empty, like usual. We were no threat to humans, but they sensed we were different and stayed away from us.

"Duh, because she's from the enemy pack." I kept my voice at a low whisper. Roane could still hear me but not the humans a few rows in front of us.

"Technically, she's not part of the pack because she's a girl. Think how epic that would be if you managed to snag their alpha's daughter!" Roane tried to be quiet, too, but he wasn't very good at it. His voice was as big as he was, and his last words came out loud enough that someone might have heard him if the second bell hadn't rung then.

"My dad thinks they're lower than dirt. He'd never allow it." I shook my head and opened my notebook, thinking that was the end of it, but Roane didn't give up as easily as I did. He was more like an alpha than I was.

"Seems like you ought to be able to make your own decisions about personal stuff like who you mate with."

I snorted. My father had picked out my future mate and made every other important decision about my life, as well. I had less say about what I could and couldn't do than anyone else in the pack.

"You know how my dad is. He expects to be the boss of everyone, especially his own kid."

"Yeah, but you're gonna be alpha someday. You should stand up for your rights." Roane crossed his meaty arms over his broad chest.

He looked more like an alpha than I did, too. I wasn't small, but Roane had 30 pounds and several inches on me. He hunched over when he was around me, trying to make himself smaller than me, but he wasn't fooling anybody.

"And risk getting my head ripped off? No thanks. As long as my dad's alpha, I have to do what he says." I turned my attention towards the teacher who was directing us to open our books to the current chapter. I flipped my book open and found the page like a dutiful student.

Ironically, being the alpha's son had made me the ultimate follower, not a leader. Maybe my mindset would change when I became alpha, but I doubted it. I'd never felt like an alpha, even though I knew I would be one eventually. I just couldn't see beyond my father's authority or imagine myself being in charge of the whole pack. It was weird enough that all the pack mates my age deferred to me and followed me around like I was already their alpha.

It would be a very long time before my father died, anyway, so I didn't have to worry about it for now. But that also meant it would be a long time before I got to make any decisions for myself, including who I dated.

An image of Tia popped into my head—Roane's sister and the girl my father wanted me to mate with for the same reason that he'd encouraged me to be friends with Roane. Their father was my dad's beta.

I didn't mind being friends with Roane, although we made an unlikely pair, and his sister was nice and pretty. But I wasn't attracted to her in that way. Not the way my eyes dilated, my throat went dry, and my heart pounded out of my chest this morning at the sight, and smell, of Luna. That was what it was supposed to feel like. How could I ever be satisfied with Tia now that I knew it could be like that with someone else?

I'd held off on dating Tia, who was only a freshman, out of respect for Roane. He knew the plan was for me to mate with her eventually but he was weirded out by the whole idea of his best friend dating his sister, like any brother would be. Was that why he was encouraging me to go for Luna?

Her face took the place of Tia's in my mind, and the memory of her scent came rushing back, intoxicating me all over again. I closed my eyes to savor the memory. When I heard myself groan, my eyes popped open.

Roane stared at me like I was making a fool of myself. I felt my cheeks heat up, and he smirked and glanced down. I threw one hand over my lap and covered my face with the other.

"You got any classes with her?" Roane whispered.

"Just one." I didn't know whether I was grateful or disappointed, but I suddenly regretted all the months I'd purposefully ignored her. Now I couldn't wait to see her again.

I spent the next two class periods in a daze, replaying every memory I had of her. Fortunately, there were quite a few of them because Luna was smart and confident and liked to speak her mind in class. She probably got that from her father. It was too bad my father's alpha personality hadn't rubbed off on me.

In European History, she sat on the opposite side of the room like she always did, but I noticed her eyes flick towards me when she walked in. I let myself watch her as she strutted to her seat, head held high, taking long strides across the room. Her unbuttoned overshirt fluttered behind her, revealing the curve of her waist in her tight tank. Her scent was even more potent than I remembered.

It wafted towards me, overwhelming me with sensations I'd never felt before and a need so strong it felt like an instinct.

I'd never paid much attention to her before, but today I couldn't take my eyes off her. She fidgeted in her seat, anxious and uncomfortable, like a young pup eager for a run. Every few minutes she looked my way.

The first time, she caught me staring at her, and I quickly dipped my head. The second time, I let our eyes connect for a second before I turned away. The third time, I held my gaze, forcing her to break the contact. There was no point hiding my interest since she obviously felt it, too.

I hung back for a minute after the bell rang, hoping maybe to talk to her on her way out, but a friend of hers caught her attention instead. She glanced at me over her friend's shoulder, though, so I had a feeling she wished she was talking to me instead. My next class was way at the other end of the building, so I couldn't stick around long. After two minutes, I reluctantly forced myself to leave.

I didn't hear a thing in my last class before lunch, all I could focus on was seeing her at lunch time. I'd have an entire free hour to catch her attention if I could find her. I had no idea what she normally did. Did she eat in the cafeteria or drive to one of the fast food restaurants nearby? Maybe she went home since she lived close.

My pack mates and I usually brought our own food and ate outside in a far corner of the school property where we had privacy to talk about pack issues and gnaw on the hunks of raw meat we liked without any strange looks. But today, as soon as the bell rang, I raced to the front doors of the school instead, hoping to spot Luna if she left the building. When she wasn't among the crowd of students who poured out of the building in the first few minutes, I decided to look for her in the cafeteria.

As soon as I entered the large room, I caught a whiff of her scent. My eyes roamed the space till they landed on her, at the back of the line, restlessly poking her head around the person in front of her as she waited in the slow-moving line. I hurried over so I could get in line behind her, hoping I had some cash on me.

She sucked in a deep breath and whipped around as soon as I got near her, like she could smell me, too. Her eyes widened, and her body stiffened as I moved within inches of her.

"Hey Luna." Another brilliant line. But her scent had turned me into a salivating animal again, with nothing on my mind but mating.

"What are you doing here?" Her eyes darted around like she wanted to run, but she stayed put.

"Getting lunch, same as you," I said, trying to act nonchalant, as I caught a glimpse of her brother from the corner of my eye, staring me down.

"You don't normally eat in here."

My eyebrows jerked up. She paid more attention to me than I thought. "What can I say? I'm a sucker for the school hamburgers. I can't pass 'em up."

The way she quirked an eyebrow, I knew she didn't buy my excuse, but she didn't press the issue.

When we got to the front of the line, Luna ordered two plain hamburgers and passed on the fries and salad. I ordered two burgers, as well, and fries I probably wouldn't eat, just so it wouldn't look like I was copying her. I wanted to offer to pay for her lunch, but when I pulled my wallet out, I realized I barely had enough to cover mine. I quickly held out some bills towards the cashier as soon as Luna finished paying then sucked up my nerve.

"Wanna sit with me?" I asked before she had a chance to head off to wherever she normally sat.

She turned and stared at me, a million questions and just as many concerns reflected in the blue pools of her eyes. But before she had a chance to answer, her brother appeared beside her and grabbed her arm, tugging her away from me. His pack mates circled around them, their scowling faces hardened, menacing.

"I told you to leave my sister alone, Nikko. You wanna start something?" Zander growled.

"Do you?" I hissed back.

CHAPTER 3

LUNA

MY BROTHER AND NIKKO STARED EACH OTHER DOWN LIKE they were about to get in a fight over me, their eyes blazing with unspoken threats. I could feel the tension sparking between them like an electric field. Zander's army of friends hovered behind him, ready to attack. I let Zander tug me away till the current between them started to dissipate. But I was still fuming.

When Nikko walked away, I yanked my arm out of Zander's strong grip, almost dropping my tray in the process. "What was that about?"

He narrowed his dark eyes at me, giving me that same look Dad always gave. "You need to stay away from Nikko. He's trouble."

I put a fist on my hip and scowled back at him. "You're not the boss of me, Zander. Don't tell me what to do."

I could tell he was about to argue with me, but instead, he said, "Dad doesn't want you anywhere near him."

I huffed and stalked off towards my usual table. As much as I felt attracted to Nikko, he did intimidate me, and his sudden interest seemed suspicious. I wasn't sure I wanted to sit with him.

I plopped down next to my friend Macy who sat, nibbling on a peanut butter and jelly sandwich. The scent of it turned my stomach. I felt a little guilty eating meat in front of her since she'd converted me to vegetarianism a few years ago, but not guilty enough to give up my burgers.

Zander waved off his group of friends and followed me then dropped his tray down beside mine with a loud clatter, garnering a strange look from Macy. Since he was so intent on making sure I didn't have any contact with Nikko, I decided to press him for answers. "What's Dad's beef with him, anyway?"

He opened his mouth then glanced at Macy, who had stopped eating to stare at us over her sandwich, her wispy, blonde hair building up static against the scarf around her neck as she flicked her head back and forth between us. Would Zander have told me the truth if she wasn't there? And why was it such a secret?

"It doesn't matter. Just stay away from him."

I rolled my eyes. Zander treated Dad's rules like the Ten Commandments, while I looked at them more like suggestions. Like speed limit signs that I could hedge a little without too much consequence.

"Who are you talking about?" Macy put down her sandwich, obviously more interested in the conversation than her boring lunch.

"Nikko Brisbane," I said at the same time Zander said, "It's none of your business."

Macy ignored Zander and shifted her attention towards me, a grin brightening her face. "Oh, he's cute.

Kind of scary, but in a hot, bad boy kind of way. Are you into him?"

I cringed. Her description of him wasn't helping the situation.

"No, I'm not," I said for Zander's benefit, although the truth was more complicated than that.

I scanned the crowd for Nikko and couldn't find him. He must've gone off to wherever his friends normally ate. I turned my attention to Zander. "You can go now. You've scared him off."

Zander looked around and must've come to the same conclusion because he stood up and picked up his tray. "Tell him to back off if he comes near you again, Luna. I mean it. There are plenty of other guys in this school. Pick someone besides him."

Zander's bossiness was really starting to irritate me, but I wanted him to scram so I could talk to Macy about Nikko. I sucked it up and said, "You don't have to worry about it. I'm not interested in him."

Zander nodded and walked off towards his own group of friends. As soon as he was out of earshot, Macy whipped her head around to gawk at me.

"What was that about?"

I'd kept my feelings about Nikko a secret from Macy because I knew she'd badger me about it if I told her, and there was no point since he never showed me the least bit of interest, anyway. But now I couldn't resist spilling. I leaned closer and grinned with a smile so big it made Macy flinch a little.

"Nikko came up to me this morning and told me I looked nice today, and in history class, he kept staring at me. Then he got behind me in the lunch line and asked me to sit with him, but Zander went all caveman on him and scared him off."

While Macy processed that information, I took the opportunity to bite off a huge chunk of my hamburger and chew it voraciously. I'd been starving all morning. I had the whole thing gone in three bites. The meat tasted pretty good, but the bun clung to the roof of my mouth like soggy cardboard. I choked it down but pulled the meat out of my second sandwich and tossed the bread aside.

Macy started talking while I chewed, spraying out words like machine gun bullets. She was so caught up in the Nikko thing, she didn't even notice I was eating meat. "Wow, were you totally stoked? I would be. He's so cool. Did you mean it when you told Zander you weren't into him?"

"No, I've actually liked him for a while, but he avoided me like the plague. I don't know what changed his mind today." I shrugged and swallowed the last of my meat, wishing I'd bought a third sandwich.

Macy gave a little pout that I hadn't told her before but quickly moved on. "Well, you do look great today. I don't know what it is, but there's something different about you."

I smiled and tossed my hair. I felt different, too. Powerful. I'd always been confident, but that day I felt like I could take on the world.

"So, what's Zander's problem with him?"

"He's just channeling my father. My dad doesn't like Nikko's family for some unknown reason, so he's always told us to stay away from them."

"That sucks.What are you going to tell him if he asks you out?"

I gave her a mischievous grin. "I'll tell him we have to keep it a secret."

She grinned back at me, her eyes lighting up. "Like Romeo and Juliet. So romantic!"

My grin turned into a scowl. "You know they both die, right?"

She pouted. "That's not the point."

We chatted for a while about Nikko's attributes and made silly speculations about why my dad didn't like his.

Maybe Nikko's dad bullied him in high school," Macy suggested.

"Or stole his girlfriend. Maybe Mrs. Brisbane was supposed to be my mom!" I teased.

"Would that mean Nikko should've been your brother?" Macy twisted her face in a quizzical look, and I couldn't tell if she was joking or being serious.

I rolled my eyes and shook my head. "Maybe it was a business deal gone bad, and my dad thinks Mr. Brisbane cheated him."

"Maybe he did. Maybe he's a criminal. Or a mob boss! Nikko does seem kind of dangerous." She wiggled her eyebrows playfully, but her words hit on my own suspicions.

My dad was tough and demanding, but he was a good person. He wouldn't dislike someone so intensely for no reason. Maybe Nikko's family was villainous and that was why he wanted me to stay away from them. I really didn't know Nikko well enough to say. I needed to find out more information before I made up my mind about him. I vowed to quiz Zander as soon as we were alone.

The day's strange events kept my mind on edge all day, and the restless energy that had been plaguing me only got worse. I wanted to run, or fight, or do something besides sit at a desk and listen to lectures. By the end of the day, I was crawling out of my skin.

Zander gave me a weird look when he got in my truck after school, like he could sense my discontent. "Did you see Nikko this afternoon?" he immediately asked.

"No." I started to tell him that I only had one class with Nikko, and it was in the morning, but I decided to kept that information to myself. The last thing I needed was for my little brother checking up on me in class. He was almost three years younger than me; I didn't know why he always thought he needed to look after me. I wasn't some wimpy little girl who needed a protector.

"What's Dad got against him and his family, anyway? What'd they ever do to him? Or you?" I turned down the stereo, hoping to get a straight answer from him now that we were alone.

But Zander sneered at me, irritated. "Can't you just do what you're told for once without questioning it?"

His words stoked a fire in me, and I let it blaze through my eyes. "No, I'm not a mindless soldier. I can think for myself and make my own decisions. Give me one good reason why I should stay away from Nikko, and don't say because Dad said so."

Zander winced and rubbed the dark stubble on top of his head. "Look, it's not my place to tell you. Just trust me, okay? You know I'm only looking out for you. And stay out of trouble this weekend while Dad and I are gone."

I pulled into the driveway and parked behind Mom's car since she never went anywhere in the evenings, leaving the other side open for Dad. "You guys are going hunting this weekend?"

"Yeah, we're leaving tomorrow after school." Zander got out, but instead of going inside, he headed towards the wooden shed in the backyard where Dad kept his shotguns and other hunting supplies. I jumped out of the truck and followed him, my boots squelching in the rain soaked yard.

I'd never been in the shed before; it was always off limits to us kids. Zander pulled his keychain out of his pocket and moved to unlock the door, but he stopped and turned to glance curiously at me when he heard me coming up behind him. I didn't know when Dad had entrusted Zander with a key. Maybe the same time he started taking him hunting with him, about a year ago.

I felt a little slighted that he'd never offered to take me with him. I'd never been too interested in Dad's monthly hunting trips before, but now that I thought about it, it sounded exactly like what I needed to work off this energy. I wanted to hike through the woods, chase after prey, and shoot off a powerful weapon.

"I want to go," I blurted out on impulse.

"What?" Zander gawked at me.

"I want to go hunting with you guys. How come you never take me?"

"Uh, cuz you're a girl."

I propped my fists on my hips. "So? Some girls like to hunt. I might be one of them. How can I know unless I try?"

"You won't like it. The woods are full of bugs and snakes and other gross stuff. It's mostly just sitting and waiting. You have to be quiet, and you're no good at that. And then you have to skin what you shoot."

It didn't sound as exciting as I imagined, but I didn't like to be told no. "I don't mind. I want to go."

Zander sighed. "Ask Dad if you want, but he'll say no. Hunting isn't for girls. Go shopping with Mom, or something."

"That's sexist and just plain wrong. I'm as capable as you are."

"This is our thing, Luna. Leave it alone."

We stared each other down for several moments before I huffed and stomped away. If I couldn't go hunting with them, I'd find some other way to entertain myself, and it wouldn't be shopping with Mom. With my dad and brother gone, there'd be no one around to stop me from going out with Nikko. I decided right then, if he asked me, I'd say yes. Or better yet, maybe I'd ask him myself.

CHAPTER 4

NIKKO

Zander flared his nostrils and whirled around to stare at me as I passed by his locker. He crossed his arms over his chest, flashing his newly developed muscles, and shot death rays at me from his eyes.

For such a young pup, Luna's brother sure wasn't afraid to stand up to me. I knew he was in line to be his pack's next alpha, but my father had always talked about their pack like they were weak and pathetic, so Zander's confidence surprised me. Either he was a lot stronger than I assumed, or he was really stupid. I was betting on the latter.

A year ago, he'd been a scrawny, little kid, but when puberty instigated that first shift, like most wolves, he bulked up quickly. All those new muscles could go to a wolf's head and make him think he was more badass than he really was.

But what was he going to do, fight me? Now that would be the ultimate stupidity. If he did, that could lead to a war between the packs, which I was almost positive his pack would lose, since, according to my father, they denied their true nature and rarely let themselves shift. They wouldn't know how to fight in wolf form.

No, Zander might talk big and blow a lot of smoke, but if I wanted to be with Luna, there was nothing he could do about it. I jumped towards him, baring my teeth and growling at him so he wouldn't think I was afraid of him. I wanted Luna, and I wasn't going to let her little brother intimidate me. He'd made it a challenge, now, and my pack didn't back down from challenges.

I didn't expect to see Luna the rest of the day which gave me plenty of time to come up with a plan for tomorrow. I'd sit next to her during history class, convince her to eat lunch with me somewhere her brother wouldn't be, then ask her to go out with me. I was pretty sure she'd say yes if Zander wasn't around to interfere.

Before I entered the house that afternoon, I could hear my dad clanking weights in the dining room he'd converted to a home gym after Mom died and we started eating our meals over the sink instead of at the table. He turned to look at me as I came in and immediately flared his nostrils then pushed the barbell up into the stand and sat up, wiping his sweat-slicked muscles that bulged like boulders under his skin. From the pungent smell coming off him, he'd been at it for a while.

"Pumping again? Didn't you work out this morning?" I asked, trying to distract him from whatever had put that angry look on his face. I should've known to pick a better topic. He launched into the same lecture he'd given me a thousand times.

"I'm the alpha. I need to be the biggest, strongest wolf

in our pack. As the next in line, you should be doing the same. You need your pack mates to respect you, fear you."

"Fine, I'll work out." It was easier to agree with him than to argue about it. I kept my shirt on because I looked puny compared to him and sat down at the pec deck machine, adjusting the weight setting he had it on by 50 pounds before starting in on butterfly presses. Dad shook his head and snorted then picked up where he left off, bench pressing the weight of a small car.

I did work out regularly, but not with the same obsession he had. Just being a wolf made me stronger and more muscular than most human guys my age, and the genes I'd inherited from my dad made me bulkier than most wolves, too. I didn't feel the need to be Hulk size like he did.

"Why do I smell the Ammon pack on you... and someone else?" he grunted between lifts.

"I was taking to Luna for a little while, and her brother got up in my craw about it. No big deal."

Hi eyes narrowed under the shaggy, brown hair that flopped, dripping with sweat, around his face. "Why were you talking to Luna?"

My face curled into a smile as the memory of her scent took over my brain. My dad saw it and slammed down his barbell with a loud clatter, vibrating the whole room.

He glared at me, and his voice got as hard as his muscles. "Why were you talking to Luna, Nikko?"

I opened my mouth, but how could I explain something I didn't understand myself? Dad got the gist of it from the lovestruck look on my face.

"Tia is your intended mate. You have no reason to go

looking for some other girl, especially not from the Ammon pack."

I kept pumping, trying to come off as nonchalant. "I'm not looking for a girlfriend, Dad. I was just hanging out with her."

He abandoned his barbell and switched to the chin-up bar. His face tensed up in a grimace, and he grunted through gritted teeth as he pulled his heavy body several feet off the floor with his massive biceps. "You have no business fraternizing with any of their pack."

I wanted to spout Roane's rebuttal about how technically girls weren't part of the pack, but I knew better than to be a smartass. He'd backhand me into the living room. Maybe I could spin it as a strategy.

"She seemed into me, so I thought maybe if I made friends with her, she might spill some insider information about their pack."

He let his body drop to the floor with a ground-shaking thud. "Don't try to pretend you're not thinking with your dick instead of your brain! She doesn't know anything useful about their pack, and you know it. If anything, she's trying to get secrets out of you."

I thought about mentioning that I'd approached her, not the other way around, but I didn't figure that would help anything. Better to kept my mouth shut, take my lumps, and let him have his say.

"Just because we have a truce with them right now doesn't make them our friends, Nikko! They'd try to take us down if they thought they could."

I scrunched my face in confusion. "I thought they were pacifists who never even shifted?"

"Are you a moron? Haven't you learned anything in

school? The biggest wars were started by people who claimed to be on the side of good. Don't believe their holier-than-thou talk for a minute. Lupin just wanted to be alpha, so he convinced half the pack that there was something wrong with being our true selves. They're no better than we are." He started pacing, working himself up into a fervor.

"That's why I work my ass off to stay strong, so I'll be ready if they try to take over our pack. But all you think about is having fun. You're willing to put your pack at risk to chase some tail. You're weak and stupid. You're nowhere near ready to be the next alpha. I don't know if you ever will be."

He slammed his fists into the punching bag, accentuating each insult. He might as well have been punching me in the chest. I knew I wasn't cut from the same cloth as him, but no matter what I did, I could never live up to his expectations. I didn't know why I bothered trying.

Thankfully, he stomped off then, too irritated to be around me. I heard him thumping around in the kitchen, pulling out some of the venison we had in the fridge and cooking it just enough to take the chill off. It smelled great since all I'd had for lunch was a couple overcooked burgers, but I wasn't about to go out there.

I did a bunch of reps to channel my anger and pacify him a little. As much as I hated it when he talked to me like that, he was probably right. It was stupid of me to go after Luna. I should stay as far away from her and her pack as possible. Like Dad said, our packs were enemies, not friends. But I couldn't stop thinking about her as I worked out, her face and scent lingering in my mind.

THE NEXT DAY, I HEADED TO SCHOOL INTENDING TO STAY far away from Luna, her brother, and any other wolves in the Ammon pack. But my resolve faltered the minute I walked in the door and caught a whiff of Luna's scent. It was stronger than yesterday, if that was even possible. I didn't see her, but my body followed the trail automatically, pulled along by an invisible tether.

I found her at her locker, talking to her friend, looking incredible in a tight, red tee shirt and black leggings. She lit up when she saw me, curling her lips in a smile and peeking over her friend's shoulder at me. Her friend caught her reaction and turned to see what she was looking at. Then she grinned and whipped back around, presumably jabbering to Luna about me since Luna kept nodding and smiling my way. I drifted towards her.

But her brother was a few steps away with his pack, keeping one eye on her, and he saw her reaction, too. He quickly glanced down the hall to see what she was looking at, his eyes glinting as they focused in on me. He kicked off from the locker he was leaning against and headed my way.

I quickly adjusted my trajectory away from Luna. When Zander got close, I mumbled, "I'm just walking down the hall, Zander. Don't start something you're not ready to finish."

He glared at me. "Oh, I'm ready, all right. Are you?"

Maybe my dad was right. Maybe they would fight us if they had a good enough reason. I could probably take Zander since he was a few years younger than me, but I didn't know enough about the rest of his pack to estimate how my own would fare against them. Besides, I'd told myself yesterday I was going to stay away from Luna. I certainly didn't want to be the one to spark a pack war. If the other pack didn't kill me, my father would.

"I'm not fighting you over your stupid sister. She's not worth it," I spat out, trying to keep from looking like a wuss. But at the same time I prayed Luna hadn't heard the insult. And it probably wasn't smart to insult a guy's sister in an attempt to defuse a fight. My dad was right about that, too: I was an idiot.

I kept walking, fast, hoping Zander wouldn't come after me. He was smart enough to know not to start a fight in the middle of school, at least. But who knew what he might try later? Hopefully he'd come to the same conclusion as me and let it drop.

By the time I got to history class, I'd re-convinced myself to stay away from Luna. When she walked in the room, I gave her a quick glance then turned away, focusing on pulling out last night's homework. I forced myself not to look up when her scent wafted towards me, making my balls tighten and my head cloud with lust.

My whole body hummed with the desire to rush towards her. I imagined myself tossing my desk and racing over to her, grabbing her and pressing her against my body, feeding the fire that ravaged me. But I clutched tightly to my chair till my fingers ached. She was just some girl; I could resist her.

When she sat down beside me, I just about exploded.

"Hey, Nikko."

My self-control disintegrated into ash, burnt up by my lust. The only thing that kept me from pouncing on her was the bar connecting my desk to my chair that penned me in and the vague thought that this wasn't exactly an appropriate place to act out my fantasies. I turned towards her, grabbing the cool, metal bar like it was my last grasp on reality.

"Hey, Luna," I croaked, holding my breath.

"Sorry about my brother. He's an ass."

"It's okay. He's just trying to protect you." She needed to be protected, because I was one sniff away from ravaging her.

"I don't need protection, and I can decide for myself who I want to hang out with. Zander and my dad are going out of town tonight. So, I was thinking, if you want, maybe you and I could…"

If I want? Did she not see that I was an inferno of desire over here? All my plans to stay away from her went up in smoke.

"Yeah, definitely. Sounds good. What time should I pick you up…" The words slipped out before I thought about what a bad idea it would be to show up on their land. Her father and brother would know in a heartbeat that I'd been there, and they'd consider it a threat. Thankfully, she threw me a bone.

"I volunteered to stay after school and help set up for the fall festival, but once it starts, I'm free. Maybe you could meet me here around 6 and we could check out the festival?"

I swallowed hard. She wanted to hang out in public, where the entire school could see us? Her brother would find out for sure. But what was I supposed to say—don't you want to go somewhere more private? She'd think I was trying to get in her pants. At least at the festival there'd be plenty of witnesses, so none of the Ammon pack could accuse me of anything untrue. Or start a wolf fight.

"Yeah, sure. Where will you be?"

"Look for me by the food tent."

The bell rang then, ending our conversation. The teacher kept us busy taking notes on his lecture, so I didn't have time to talk any more with Luna. Although, her scent kept me in an agitated state of arousal the whole time.

When class was over, she gave me a little smile and a wave before taking off. I wanted to walk her to her next class, but maybe it was better that I didn't. Her brother and his pack mates might see us. Better to keep things on the down low as long as possible.

At lunch, I didn't bother looking for her. Her scent was too much temptation. Maybe it was for the best that our date was out in public. Otherwise, I wouldn't trust myself to keep my hands off her. But being with her and not touching her was going to be torture.

CHAPTER 5

LUNA

WHAT WAS WRONG WITH ME? PEOPLE TALKED ABOUT teenage boys being obsessed with sex, but I couldn't imagine anyone feeling hornier than I was. I felt like a raging ball of fire, burning up with need. My whole body ached with it. Since I couldn't have sex, I wanted to run or fight or do something wild and aggressive. Setting up the condiment table in the food tent was definitely not satisfying any of my urges.

I squeezed the dispenser a few times to prime the pump till mustard squirted out onto my sausage sandwich. Then I took a giant bite, hoping to curb at least one of my appetites. It was the closest thing to release I'd gotten all day.

I hadn't given much thought to sex before, but then, I'd never been interested in any guy besides Nikko, and I didn't think anything would ever happen between us. Now, it was all I could think about. But it wasn't only Nikko I was thinking about. My libido revved up whenever I got near any of his group.

My brother's friends had the same effect on me, but I couldn't bring myself to think about them like that. I'd known them since they were little kids. None of the other guys in school interested me at all, though. That seemed weird.

But then, the whole thing was. I felt like my body had been taken over by space invaders, and I wasn't in control of myself anymore. What had changed? I had no idea, but there was nobody I felt comfortable talking to about it.

My mother was too much of a Pollyanna. Any talk like that would probably humiliate her. Talking to my Dad or brother would humiliate me. That left Macy, but she didn't have any experience either, as far as I knew. And she seemed much more interested in the causes she championed than getting laid.

When Nikko showed up, I shoved the last bite of sausage into my mouth, hoping he wouldn't see that I'd been eating already. He'd probably want to get something to eat later, and I knew I'd be hungry again. My stomach had been just as needy lately as my sex drive. I didn't want him to think I was a pig.

I surreptitiously wiped my fingers across my mouth in case there was any lingering mustard then dropped my hand so he could see my megawatt smile. His was just as big. Could it be true? Could he be just as into me as I was him?

He smelled great, even better than the sausage they were cooking, like he was putting off pheromones designed to lure me in. I didn't need them. He looked great, too, in snug, dark jeans and a burgundy shirt that complimented his dusky, olive skin and made his amber eyes pop. They seemed extra bright that night, with the string of lights draped across the food tent sparkling in them. They gazed into mine, hypnotizing me for a moment.

He reached out a hand towards me, and I glanced down at it, breaking the spell. But before I could process what he wanted, he pulled it back and shoved it in his pocket. My body started screaming, "Please, touch me!" It sounded so loud inside my head, he had to have heard it, but all he did was move close enough to build up a crackling heat between our bodies. I forced myself to ignore it and focus on what he was saying.

"Do you want to walk around a bit, see what's here?"

I nodded and let him lead me out of the food tent, our shoulders brushing, setting off sparks that I was sure were visible in the darkness. Thankfully, the chilly, fall air cooled my overheated skin. Otherwise, I might've ignited. A crowd of people flowed around us, chattering, and barkers shouted at us from brightly lit, carnival-style game booths that lined both sides of the path. But all I could concentrate on was being next to Nikko.

"I feel like I've known you forever, but I don't know that much about you. What do you like to do?" His question yanked me out of my daze.

"I'm the captain of the girls' basketball team, and I'm on the debate team."

He chuckled. "Why doesn't that surprise me?"

I elbowed him and made a face. "What, you think I'm a know-it-all?"

He held up his hands and shook his head, but his grin that told me that he did, at least a little. Maybe I was a bit opinionated. "No, no. But you always have something to say in class, and you hold your own against your brother."

"He likes to boss people around, but it doesn't work on me."

That comment prompted a curious look that made me wonder what he was thinking. I had no clue, because I knew almost nothing about him, either. Was I only attracted to him because of his looks and the fact that I wasn't supposed to be? I hoped not; that sounded so shallow. I quickly changed the subject to him so I could find some reason to like him besides how sexy he was.

"What about you? What do you like to do?"

"Hang out with my friends. Run track. I workout a lot."

As soon as he said that, he blushed and dipped his head. "I didn't mean it like that."

I put a hand on his arm. "No, don't be modest. It's obviously true."

I couldn't resist squeezing his firm bicep. He peeked up at me and grinned. That small touch was nowhere near enough contact to satisfy me, but short of launching myself at him, it was the most I could get. I thought about reaching for his hand, but I didn't want to make the first move.

"So, when will your dad and brother be back?"

His question put all kinds of thoughts in my head. Was he already thinking about spending more time with me? I'd never been more grateful for their monthly hunting trips than at that moment. It meant my whole weekend was free to spend with Nikko if he wanted to.

"Not till Sunday night. They went hunting up in the Razorback Hills. They go about once a month." I tossed that in so he'd know that we'd have other opportunities to be together without my brother breathing down our necks. You know, just in case.

Nikko stiffened and turned to me, his eyes wide. He looked pale, but maybe that was just an effect of the moonlight. "Whenever there's a full moon?"

"Yeah. Dad says that's his favorite time to hunt. How'd you know? Do you hunt, too?"

"Yeah, sometimes." He started walking again. I scurried to catch up with him.

"Do you ever go to the Razorback Hills?"

He flicked his eyes towards me. "No, I never go there."

"Maybe you should try it. It must be a good place since my Dad always hunts there."

He stopped and gave me a serious look. "Don't tell him you told me that. Hunters don't like to give up their secret spots."

I winced and let the subject drop. Nikko got quiet after that, making me wonder if I'd upset him. Worries ping-ponged around in my brain. Had I screwed things up between us already?

After we'd walked the whole circuit, Nikko stopped and said, "I'm getting hungry. Want to eat?"

The one sausage sandwich I'd eaten hadn't satisfied me, so I nodded eagerly. We went back to the food tent and scarfed down a few more. Nikko passed on the bun, so I did, too. His contemplative mood lightened, and soon we were making sausage jokes that gave me inappropriate thoughts. After we were done eating, we headed back out to the midway.

"What would you like to do next?"

"Um, whatever you want. I don't care." I knew I sounded brainless, but I couldn't focus on anything but the lust burning in my veins and my edgy restlessness.

"Want to play one of the games?" Nikko asked.

I glanced around for a moment at the choices. When my eyes landed on a couple clinging to each other, hopping in the three-legged race, my body went haywire, imagining us tangled up together.

"How about that one?" I pointed.

Nikko looked at me and smiled like he could read my mind. A blush crept up my neck and flared in my cheeks, but I was too caught up in his stare to drop my head.

"Let's do it."

We joined the group waiting for the next round. When it was our turn, the game leader tied a bandana around our ankles. Nikko and I immediately clung to each other to keep our balance. His hip pressed against mine, and his hand wrapped around my waist, pinning me to him. My heart sped up, making me breathe harder even though we hadn't started yet.

When the whistle blew, we took off faster than all the others. His strong legs took long steps in time with my pounding heart, but I managed to keep up with him, clinging to his taut abs. My shirt rode up as we moved, and his fingers filled the gap, searing my skin.

Despite the fact that my thoughts were all focused on the feel of his body touching mine, we crossed the finish line first. As soon as we did, I pumped my fists in the air in a victory hoot, but letting go knocked us both off balance, and we tumbled to the ground in a heap.

Nikko landed on top of me, his firm, muscular body hot and heavy but pressing in all the right places. When he started to get up, I held on, pulling him tighter against me till he got the hint and stopped moving. His face hovered over mine, his warm breath on my skin, his golden eyes glowing like firelight, mesmerizing me.

I lifted my head just enough to brush my lips against his. As soon as I did, he moaned and took over, devouring me with his lips. Desire exploded in my mouth and shot through my body, electrifying every nerve till I sparked and quivered like a downed wire. I dug my nails into his back, and he writhed against me like my touch had completed the circuit, sending the electricity flowing through him, too.

A loud throat-clearing distracted me just long enough for me to realize we were making a spectacle of ourselves. Nikko must've realized it, too, because he jumped up, at least as much as he could since our legs were tied together. My body instantly complained at the loss of him.

"Let's get out of here," I whispered, my voice rough, needy.

He nodded and quickly untied us. The game leader tried to give us a prize, but we ignored her and hurried off. As soon as we got away from the crowds, Nikko stopped and turned to me, his face contorted in guilt.

"I'm sorry, Luna. I shouldn't have done that. Do you want to go home?"

"No, of course not! What are you apologizing for. I wanted it." I only paused for a second before blurting out the truth. "I want more."

"You do?"

Instead of answering him, I threw myself at him. He caught me and held me by the waist as I plundered his mouth with my lips and tongue. He gave back as good as he got, sucking and nipping at my lips, his fingers stroking up and down my sides, drawing streaks of pleasure. I squirmed against him, desperate for more contact even though almost every inch of our bodies was touching.

I pulled away just long enough to say, "Let's go in the woods."

Nikko's eyes got so wide, I could see more white than color. "The woods?"

"Yeah, it's the only place that's private."

Nikko gaped at me as I darted over to my truck and pulled a blanket out from behind the seat, part of the emergency kit my dad had insisted I carry when I inherited the old truck that was prone to breaking down. The fabric felt rough and pilled from a lifetime of washings.

"What's that for?"

"It's not great, but it's better than lying directly on the ground." In my desperate state, I was surprised I'd thought of it.

"The ground?" Nikko stumbled after me as I tromped into the trees beside the parking lot. The woods quickly engulfed us, blocking out the light and much of the sound from the festival. In the stillness, all I could hear was our heavy breathing and the crackle of leaves crunching under our feet. Nikko's scent seemed stronger out there, a musky, animal smell layered on top of the earthy scent of the forest.

As soon as we'd gone far enough that no one could spot us, I searched for a clear spot where I could spread out the blanket. Once I found one, I shook the blanket out and let it float to the ground. Moonlight filtered through the trees, illuminating the setting with a pale glow, making an old blanket in the woods seem almost romantic. I dropped down onto it and reached for Nikko's hand to pull him down next to me, but he didn't budge.

"Luna, are you sure? You don't have to do this." His voice was tentative but husky with desire.

A small voice in the back of my head told me I was crazy, that I was a wanton slut who was about to give it up on my first date, and that Nikko didn't want me that way. But the bulge in his pants proved the latter wasn't true, and my body was too lust-crazed for me to care about anything else. I had to quench this fire inside me now.

"Yes I do, Nikko. I'm going to explode if I don't. Please." I begged him with my eyes and my voice to give me what I wanted, needed, and for half a second I felt guilty about manipulating him. But the look in his eyes told me he wanted it just as badly as I did.

He nodded and dropped to his knees beside me. I lunged for him, knocking him backwards and pressing my body on top of his, trying to ease my need. He stroked me, leaving a trail of fire everywhere his hands touched. We kissed and writhed against each other for a few minutes till I jerked myself upright and yanked my shirt over my head. I unhooked my bra and tossed it aside, as well. The cool air instantly pebbled my nipples.

"You're gorgeous, Luna." Nikko reached out to touch me, and I moaned and let my head loll back as his fingers kneaded my tender, aching flesh. No one had ever touched me there, and it felt amazing.

Eventually, I pushed his shirt up so I could stroke his taut abs. The moonlight cast shadows that emphasized the contours of his fit body. I unbuttoned his jeans and ran my fingers down the ridges that disappeared below his waistband. Even though I could feel his hardness through the thin material of my leggings, I still wanted more contact, so I stood up and pushed them down to my ankles, kicking off my Chucks.

Nikko shimmied out of his own pants, never taking his eyes off me. Flames licked up my body as his eyes trailed up and down me. I swear, steam was curling off me.

I'd never gone this far with a guy before. I'd never done anything, really. So, I flinched when Nikko grabbed his discarded pants and dug a condom out of his wallet. I didn't want to think about him with other girls, but I guess I was glad he was prepared, since I wasn't.

A minute later, he reached for my hands and guided me down onto him. I'd heard that the first time could be painful, but my body was ready for him. I quickly took control, taking what I needed from him, frantically clawing at him and moaning. I was too caught up in the pleasure to be embarrassed. When I came, my body exploded.

My skin was suddenly too tight for me, and my body ripped through it. A scream ripped from my throat at the same time. My back arched, my limbs contorted, and my mouth split wide. I threw my head back and howled like a wild animal. It was agony, like every muscle was tearing, and every bone was breaking, but I had never felt more alive, more powerful.

My body was a cage, and I'd finally escaped from it. I felt like a butterfly emerging from its chrysalis, but Nikko gaped at me like I'd turned into a monster. What was happening to me?

He only stared at me for a moment, though, before his own body exploded in front of my eyes. One second he was a naked, teenage boy, and the next he was a giant wolf, covered in thick fur that shined like strands of silver in the moonlight.

He immediately pounced on me, knocking me down, then mounted me from behind. I was too stunned to move. He howled as he came, a loud, terrifying, animal sound that echoed through the forest, scaring flocks of birds away. Then his mouth clamped onto my neck and he bit, his sharp canines piercing through my own thick fur and skin, drawing blood.

I howled at that and tore myself free, knocking him off me. All I knew to do was run, so I did, taking off into the forest. My legs bounded over fallen limbs with ease, my body darted around rocks and trees like a graceful dance. In moments, I'd traveled halfway through the forest.

The indistinguishable shapes of the dark woods crystallized before me into distinct shades of gray, every object clearly defined now. My sense of smell and hearing were amplified, too. I heard every twig crack beneath my feet, smelled every trail left by other animals. Instinct told me to hunt them down and devour them, but the part of me that was still human told me to keep running.

"Luna!" I heard Nikko's voice calling my name over and over. I wanted to run away from it, but I couldn't locate it. It was only after he pounced on me again that I realized it was in my head.

CHAPTER 6

NIKKO

I NEVER WOULD'VE BELIEVED IT IF I HADN'T SEEN IT WITH my own eyes. Luna was a werewolf! The first female one in generations. And I'd just claimed her. Could this night get any better? I couldn't help the feeling of power that rose up inside me. But I had to catch her before she did something stupid, like show herself to humans.

She was terrified and freaking out, for sure. Most werewolves were educated about their true nature long before their first shift. But I was almost positive Luna didn't know werewolves existed, let alone that she was one.

I took off into the woods after her, my strong legs eating up the forest. She was fast, but I was faster. And I'd had a lot more practice being a wolf. I followed her scent and the sound of her footfalls as she bounded though the woods. Her scent was even more intense to my wolf nose, if that was possible. But now I understood why I was so drawn to her all of a sudden. She was in heat.

No wonder she'd been insatiable. Here I thought I was

so hot she couldn't resist me. But she probably would've mated with any wolf she could get her hands on. I guess I should be grateful it was me and not one of my other pack mates. That would've upset the balance of power for sure.

It only took a few moments for me to catch up with her. I called out to her with my mind so I wouldn't scare her, and I could tell she heard it by the way her ears perked and she whipped her head around, looking for me. But she didn't understand wolf telepathy, and she wouldn't stop running. We were dangerously close to the edge of the woods, so the only thing left to do was jump on her.

"Luna, it's Nikko. Calm down; I'm not going to hurt you, but you need to listen to me."

She yelped and flailed, snapping at me with her teeth, trying to toss me off her, but I wrapped my jaws around her neck and held on tight, trying not to pierce the skin again. Eventually, she flopped to the ground, whimpering, and buried her snout in her paws.

"I'm going to let go of you, but you can't run. You're almost out of forest. You can't go out on the road where someone might see you. You promise you won't take off?"

She whined then let out a pathetic howl. I took that as a yes and slowly eased off her. She jumped up and shook out her fur then looked at me with anger and a million questions in her eyes.

"You can talk to me. Just think what you want to say and direct it at me."

Sometimes it takes new wolves a few tries to get the hang of it, but her thoughts came through loud and clear, maybe because they were so fierce. "What the hell is happening?! What did you do to me? Why am I a freaking wolf? Why are you a wolf?"

I tried to keep my voice calm and even, hoping she'd settle down. "I didn't do this to you. It's genetic. Our fathers are werewolves. The full moon instigated your change."

She barked and started pacing, her tail wagging erratically. "You mean my parents knew about this? It would've been nice if somebody would've warned me!"

"Well, see, no one thought to because you're the first female wolf any of us have ever seen." And more beautiful than I could've imagined. Fur just as black and lustrous as her human hair covered her lean body and shone in the moonlight. Her brilliant blue eyes, white teeth, and pink tongue stood in sharp contrast.

She sat on her haunches and stared at me. In our wolf form, we didn't give much thought to our appearance, but I'd seen my reflection in moonlit water, so I knew what my wolf looked like. What did she think when she saw me like this? Was she disgusted by me?

"Why?"

"A long time ago, male werewolves started mating with human women. Their sons were all wolves, but none of their daughters were. Eventually, there were no more female wolves around to mate with."

She chuffed and jumped up again. "So, not only am I a freak, I'm a freak among freaks?"

"No, it's not like that. You're… a miracle." I padded towards her and nuzzled my snout into her neck.

She let me for a moment then jerked her head up. "What about my mother?"

"She's human. I doubt she knows anything about this."

"You don't know for sure?"

I took a few steps away from her to think about how to explain it. There was no way to sugarcoat it. Eventually, I spit it out, but like a coward I kept myself turned away from her. "Our families belong to different packs. Opposing packs."

She bounded over to look me in the eye. "Is that why my father always told me to stay away from you?"

"And why your brother wanted to pummel me every time I got near you."

"My brother's a wolf, too?" She plopped back down on her belly on the rough forest floor, overwhelmed. I stretched out next to her. Her scent still tempted me to mate with her. Hopefully she'd be willing to let me again, eventually.

"So, is that why they go hunting every month on the full moon, so they can... shift?"

"Most likely, although, my pack believed that they never shifted until you told me about their monthly trips."

"Why?"

"Your father and several other wolves split off from my dad's pack a long time ago. They didn't think it was right for us to let our wolves out just to hunt for sport."

"So, wolves don't have to shift."

"You can learn to control it, resist the call of the moon. You can learn to shift at other times, too."

She lifted her head and sniffed, catching a whiff of a nearby deer. "What do you hunt?"

"Whatever we want, but our natural prey are vampires."

She shook her head, ruffling her fur. "Vampires! You've got to be kidding me."

I chuffed out the wolf version of a laugh. "No, they're real, too. But there are very few of them left, as far as we know. My dad saw one years ago, but I never have."

She dropped her head to the ground again and covered her eyes with her paws, whining.

"I know it's a lot to take in. Most wolves don't learn about it all this way."

Eventually, she uncovered her eyes and looked at me again, the blue orbs clouded. "So, how do I shift back?"

"You'll learn how to control that, too, eventually. But for now, you probably won't be able to until the full moon wanes."

She dug her claws into the ground and leapt up, leaving deep gouges in the dirt. "I have to stay like this all weekend? What am I supposed to tell my mother?"

"Nothing. We don't tell the women. They're not part of this world. You can't go back home till you're human again. I can shift back and use your phone to send her a text, telling her you want to spend the night at your friend's house. Will she buy that?"

She nodded, but fear glistened in her eyes.

I got up and pressed my flank against hers. "I'll stay with you, help you hunt for food."

I prayed that she wouldn't push me away. She was my claimed mate now, though she didn't know anything about that yet. My protective instincts had kicked in, and it would be torture for me to be apart from her. I'd have to tell her soon, but I didn't want to add any more to her plate right then.

Her stomach growled, and I took the opportunity to distract her from her worries. "Come on, let's hunt. Can you smell anything?"

She raised her snout and sniffed loudly then whipped her head towards a scent trail. Before I had a chance to instruct her, she took off in that direction. She was too loud, crashing through the woods, her paws pounding heavily, but she still managed to snag an opossum. She shook it in her jaw then plopped down to devour it.

"Do you like it?" I thought she might be grossed out by eating raw meat, but she didn't seem to mind at all.

"I've been starving for the last few days, and all I've wanted was meat."

"That's normal. That's all we eat mostly."

"But I'm a vegetarian."

I couldn't help but laugh. She glowered at me but kept gnawing.

"There was something else around that smelled better, but I couldn't catch it."

"Probably a deer, but you have to be a lot less conspicuous to catch them. I'll teach you."

When she was finished eating, she wiped her muzzle on her paws and yawned. "I'm exhausted, but I'm still hungry. All these cravings are driving me crazy."

"What else are you craving?" I had a suspicion, because I was craving the same thing.

Wolves don't blush, but she might as well have, the way she dropped her eyes and dipped her head.

"I think you're in heat; that's why you feel that way."

"How do you know anything about that?" She sounded mortified.

"You've been pumping out pheromones since yesterday. It took every ounce of my self-control not to jump you the minute you walked into school."

Her muzzle fell open, and she whipped around so I

couldn't see her face. I padded over to her and nuzzled her. She snapped at me.

"Don't be embarrassed. It's natural."

"So, the only reason you're interested in me is because I smell good all of a sudden?"

"What? No!"

"Then why did you act like I didn't exist before then?"

I sighed. I really didn't want to get into this again. "Opposing packs, remember?"

I wanted to forget all about our feuding families for a while and just enjoy my time with her. But in typical girl fashion, she couldn't let it drop. "So, are you going to get in trouble for being with me?"

I didn't know the answer to that. How would our fathers respond when they found out that Luna was a wolf and I'd mated with her? Had I just instigated a pack war?

CHAPTER 7

LUNA

"We don't have to tell anyone. That way, you won't get in trouble for being with me, and I won't get in trouble for being with you." That seemed like the easiest solution to me. What our parents didn't know wouldn't hurt them, and I wanted to forget that any of this had happened.

Nikko let out a whine and started pacing, his silver tail swishing nervously. "I wish it was that simple, Luna, but your dad's going to know what happened as soon as he gets one whiff of you."

"He'll know I shifted?"

"And that you were claimed."

I didn't know what that meant, but I didn't like the sound of it, and Nikko wouldn't look at me. I padded over to him and butted him with my muzzle. "Claimed? What do you mean, claimed?"

He looked at me then, angst in his golden eyes. "After you shifted, I mounted you and bit you, and you let me. It means you belong to me now, as my mate."

I tossed my head back and let out a distressed howl that echoed through the forest so loudly, my father could probably hear me up in the Razorback Hills. "What? I don't belong to you! Why would you do that? You had no right!"

All of a sudden, I wasn't attracted to him anymore; I wanted to rip his head off. I bared my teeth in a growl.

He whimpered and backed up. "It was an instinct, Luna. I couldn't help myself any more than you could help wanting to mate with me."

"So, what, you own me now?"

"It's not like that. More like we belong to each other." He nuzzled me and rubbed his flank up against mine, but I snapped my teeth at him.

"I don't want to belong to anyone, especially not someone who's only interested in me because of pheromones and instinct." I leapt over a fallen log and darted away.

Not once had Nikko said anything about liking me for me. I was just some kind of wolf conquest to him. I didn't need him, I had no desire to be mated to him, whatever that meant, and now that I knew my own attraction to him was nothing more than instinct, I could control my urges and resist him.

I didn't know anything about my own pack, but I felt a loyalty to it. I shouldn't have been fraternizing with the enemy. Why hadn't I listened to my father and stayed away from Nikko in the first place?

I ran hard, trying to get away from him. But the farther I ran, the more I felt an invisible tether tugging at me. It stretched and tightened the faster I ran, but Nikko kept after me, chasing me through the woods, calling my name in his mind.

"Luna, wait! Let's just talk a minute. I want to help you. We're in this together."

That did it. I stopped running and whirled to face him as he crashed towards me. He skidded to a stop when I came into his view, my teeth bared, saliva dripping.

"We're not together, Nikko. I don't care what kind of claim you think you have on me! You took advantage of my ignorance, but I won't let you do that again. Stay away from me. I mean it!"

I took off again, and this time he let me go. I kept running for a while till exhaustion forced me to stop. My chest heaved in painful spasms as I panted, my tongue lolling out the side of my mouth.

Over my heavy breathing, I could hear water gurgling in the distance, so I followed the sound till I spotted a little creek. I dipped my snout in the cold water and lapped at it till my thirst abated and my heartbeat settled some. Then I slumped down beside it to rest.

What was I going to do? I didn't know how to shift back, and if Nikko was to be believed, I might not be able to till the full moon waned. Would I have to stay like this, alone in the woods, all weekend?

I heard a piece of wood snap nearby and flinched. What else was out here in the dark with me? I suppose I looked like a ferocious animal to anything that saw me, but I still felt like a teenage girl inside. My fur quivered as tremors wracked my body. I buried my snout in my paws and whimpered.

I wanted my mom, but she couldn't help me. I couldn't

even tell her about this. My father had always given a lot more attention to my brother, but I wished he were here. He'd understand and know what to do, at least. Even having Zander here would be better than no one. I almost wanted to call Nikko back, but I wouldn't let myself on principle.

What was my father going to say when he found out his enemy's son had some kind of wolfy claim on me? He was going to kill me, or Nikko, or maybe both of us. He could kill Nikko for all I cared, but I wanted to live a little longer.

I was just as angry that I had to find out about the whole thing this way, but I guess he never expected me to find out at all. Now that I had more time to think about it, I couldn't get over the fact that my dad and brother had hid this huge secret from my mom and me all these years. Talk about skeletons in the closet. I felt like an idiot. How had I not noticed that my dad was a werewolf?

I didn't know where else to go, so I stayed by the brook that night, curled up in a ball. My fur kept me fairly warm. My nerves were wound tight, so every sound set me on edge, but eventually I fell into a restless slumber. I woke at sunrise, caught a rabbit for breakfast, then explored the woods a bit more. They seemed much less ominous in the daylight.

Maybe I should run away. If what Nikko said was true, no one would believe him that I had turned into a wolf. I could live in the woods, drink from the creek, and catch my own food. I wouldn't have to worry about angry parents, enemy packs, or living as a human who risked turning into a wolf at any moment.

I was seriously contemplating it, but by Sunday afternoon, loneliness had crept in. I couldn't imagine living the rest of my life as an animal with no human interaction. I didn't want to be a wolf. I liked my human life. And as much as my parents favored Zander, I knew they loved me and would be devastated if I disappeared on them. My mother was probably already worried about me, unless Nikko used my phone to text her like he suggested.

I searched the woods till I found the spot where my life had changed. The old blanket was still spread out on the ground, my clothes folded in a neat pile. Nikko's clothes were missing. I pawed through my clothes, looking for my cell phone, and found it hidden between my shirt and my leggings. I wanted to see if he'd sent any texts, but I couldn't work the phone with my paws.

I still hadn't shifted back, and I didn't know how to get home without anyone seeing me. I curled up on the blanket, my nose buried in my clothes, missing the familiarity of my old life. Even if I went home, nothing would ever be the same again.

CHAPTER 8

NIKKO

I SHOULD'VE KNOWN THAT THINKING WITH MY DICK WOULD get me in trouble. But had I just made the shrewdest move ever, or the dumbest? Either way, I was pretty sure I was going to suffer for it.

I'd claimed the first female wolf in centuries, stealing that prize from the enemy pack, no less. But I'd bound myself to a mate who wanted nothing to do with me, which meant dealing with the pain of losing her or risking a pack war to keep her.

She should've been feeling some serious attachment to me as her mate, like I was to her, but her anger was overpowering it. As much as I wanted to stay with her and help her through her first shift, I didn't want to drag her back to my cave like a Neanderthal, so I let her go, hoping she'd come to her senses eventually.

But now I had to face my dad, and that never turned out well for me.

I shifted back to my human form and headed home,

hoping he'd headed off already and I could have a few days by myself to think. But of course, I wasn't that lucky.

He, and half our pack, congregated in front of our house in wolf form, a forest of brown, gray, black, white, and russet fur with luminescent eyes glimmering in the yellow moonlight. My giant, silver father towered over them in stature and power. Great, now I had to have this confrontation in front of an audience.

I drove my SUV up the dirt drive to our home, a large, log cabin–style house set back deep on ten acres of woodland. Dad howled at me as I climbed out. In human form, I couldn't hear his thoughts, but I knew him well enough to know what he was saying. He wanted me to join the pack on their hunt.

I knew he'd smell me right away, there was no point delaying the inevitable. So as soon as I got out of the car, I yanked off my clothes to avoid shredding them then shifted. Getting naked in front of the whole pack was something you got over quickly. Besides, I wanted to keep the clothes I'd worn on the night I claimed my mate. It was a special moment, even if it would potentially bring me more pain than pleasure.

Sure enough, my dad took one whiff and stalked over towards me, baring his teeth and growling, his black eyes flashing. The wind caught my scent and carried it across the field, exciting the pack. They mewled and yipped and howled at each other, recognizing the scent of a wolf that had mated but not the scent of Luna.

"You mated with Luna Ammon. After I told you to stay away from her. How dare you dishonor your pack, and your intended, like that?" Dad broadcast his thoughts for everyone to hear, announcing my sin, but it didn't matter.

The rest of the pack could already smell that I'd mated with someone other than Tia.

It was what I had to say that shocked everyone. "She's a wolf. I saw her shift with my own eyes."

The pack exploded with barks and howls that echoed around the open area surrounding the house and scared off all the creatures in the woods beyond. An owl hooted in complaint at the commotion. The sounds inside the wolves' heads were even more chaotic as everyone expressed their disbelief and contemplated what that meant for our pack and our kind.

My father was the first to recover his composure. He moved closer to take another smell, running his snout up and down my form, growling softly as his nose confirmed the truth. I'd hoped that revelation would distract everyone for a little while, but of course, my father cut straight to the chase.

"You mated with her. Did you claim her?"

"Yes."

Another excited clamor rose up from the pack, but I held my breath, waiting for my father's response. A glimmer of pride twinkled in his eye, and his scowl softened. But it only lasted for a moment before his look hardened again.

"Where is she then?"

A defeated whine escaped my mouth before I clamped it shut. I wanted to bury my head under my paws to block out all the stares, but I didn't dare let myself look any weaker than my words were about to. I tried to make myself sound compassionate instead.

"She didn't know anything about wolves. She didn't understand what was happening. She needed some space."

"So you let her go?" He snarled. The fiery look he gave me melted my legs. I dropped to my belly in submission and whimpered.

"Mating with a she-wolf will produce a line of wolves stronger and more powerful than we've seen in generations. You were wise to claim her. That was the kind of bold action an alpha would take."

His words rang out for the whole pack to hear. A ray of pride lit my face, and I lifted my head towards it, but his next words blocked it out. He couldn't let me bask in it for one minute.

"But releasing her just because she doesn't want to be claimed? That's a pathetic display of weakness. You need to find her and bring her back. She belongs to this pack now. I expect her to be here when we return."

With that, he barked out a command, and the pack took off into the woods in a loud shuffle of pounding paws, clamoring yips and howls, and rustling branches that lasted for just a moment before the silence of the night took over again.

Great. I had the time alone I wanted but an impossible ultimatum to meet. There was no way I could convince Luna to join our pack voluntarily in a few days. I had to try, though, because forcing her to would ruin any chance of salvaging our relationship.

I was exhausted from the events of the evening, and I was sure Luna was, too, so I headed to bed, hoping she'd be calmer in the morning. But by midday Saturday I still hadn't come up with a plan for how to persuade her to leave her home and family, join an enemy pack, and spend the rest of her life as my mate. She would hate everything about that, and I didn't blame her. But I'd never live down the shame with my dad and my pack if I didn't.

On Sunday, I forced myself to look for her, even though I had no better idea what to say to her. I drove to the school and saw her truck in the parking lot, so I figured she hadn't shifted back yet and was still hiding out in the woods, probably scared and lonely. Maybe that would work in my favor.

She might be so happy to see someone that she'd forget she was mad at me. I snorted at my own ridiculous fantasy. Even as little as I knew about Luna, I was pretty sure she wanted to rip my head off.

I parked my truck next to hers and headed into the woods. I found her curled up on the nubby, brown blanket where we'd mated, still in wolf form. Just seeing her again made the tension inside me loosen and my whole body relax. I hadn't realized how strong the bond between mates was.

She jerked awake, growling in warning, then snarled when she realized who it was. I held up my hands and took a step backwards, worried she'd attack me. I could shift quickly, but if she got in a bite before I did, she could tear open my human body.

"Hey Luna, relax. I just want to talk to you." I slowly pulled off my clothes. She watched intently. The scent of her estrus still surrounded her, turning me on. Was that appreciation flashing in her eyes, or just wariness?

She jumped when I shifted and let out a howl. I quickly sat down on my haunches and whined to let her know I meant no harm. She chuffed and growled but didn't try to attack me, so I took that as a good sign.

"How are you doing? Are you okay?"

"Besides the fact that I'm stuck as a wolf, I'm fine. You don't have to worry about me."

It was on the tip of my tongue to say, "Yes, I do; you're my mate," but I bit it back.

"Do you need some food or water? I could bring you something, if you'd like."

"I found a stream and caught a rabbit. I'm good."

"Oh, okay."

She glared at me. "You can leave now."

When I didn't move, she rolled her eyes. "What do you want, Nikko?"

I sighed. So much for buttering her up. "I went home, and my dad smelled you on me. He knows we mated."

She chuffed. "I'm sure he's very proud of you."

"The thing is, since I claimed you, there are certain… expectations."

"Like what?"

I winced. There was no easy way to say it. "You're expected to join my pack and live with me as my mate."

She jumped up and threw back her head, bellowing out a howl loud enough that the entire town must've heard it. Hunters would probably be out searching the woods for big game soon. I rubbed up against her flank, nipping at her gently, trying to get her to calm down.

She growled and snapped at me, her long, white teeth dripping with saliva. She missed, but not on purpose. I backed away and let her wear herself out.

Eventually, she stopped barking and howling and stalked towards me, her pretty blue eyes ice cold with malice. "Are you insane? I barely know you! The only thing I know about your pack is that my father hates them."

I wanted to assure her that her father's hate was unjustified, but the truth was, my father could be heartless and ruthless. I didn't blame Lupin for breaking off and forming his own pack, even if I didn't agree with his reasons. But now that I knew he still shifted, I suspected it was just an excuse to escape my father's rule.

I tried to focus on the positives. "Our fathers didn't get along, but my dad won't be alpha forever. I'm next in line. And since you're a wolf, our offspring will be the strongest in generations."

"Our offspring? I'm seventeen years old! You expect me to what, marry you and start having your puppies?" She snarled again, clawing the blanket to shreds, and I didn't have the guts to tell her she might already have a pup on the way after our mating.

"We might be able to delay that for a while, but you need to join my pack. I can't let my mate live with another pack."

"I'm not your mate, Nikko. I don't care what you say. And I'm sure as hell not moving in with you and joining your pack. Just leave me alone. I don't ever want to see you again."

She started to run away, but I loped after her. "Luna, we are mated, whether you like it or not. It's the way of our kind. Don't you feel it? You can't run away from it."

"Wanna bet?" She took off, bounding through the woods at top speed.

I called after her, "Even if you tried, since you're the only female wolf around, my father isn't going to let you go without a fight."

She skittered to a stop then whipped around and growled at me. "Are you threatening me?"

"It's just the way it is."

"Well, I don't back down from a fight." She took off again, but I didn't chase her. As much as I dreaded returning without her, I wouldn't be the one to force her into something she didn't want.

CHAPTER 9

LUNA

I RACED AWAY FROM NIKKO AS FAST AS I COULD RUN, but he didn't chase after me. His words did, though. I knew nothing about pack laws, or mating, or anything, but they couldn't honestly expect me to leave my family just because Nikko claimed me as his mate. Could they?

According to Nikko, they could. Would his family really start a fight with mine over me? I needed to go home and talk to my father. He'd know what to do.

I waited till long after sunset, when most people would be asleep, to venture out of the woods. Still, I took the back way home, keeping myself as hidden as possible. Even if I looked like a regular wolf like Nikko did, I didn't want to just stroll down the street where anyone could see me.

When I got to my house, the lights were out, and Dad's pickup sat in the driveway. What was I supposed to do now, ring the bell? What if my mother answered? She'd have a heart attack. Should I wait for my dad to leave for work in the morning? I didn't want to show myself in daylight, though. We had neighbors.

I paced around the backyard for a few minutes, thinking, till eventually I whined in frustration. But that gave me an idea. Maybe if I howled, my dad would come outside to see what, or who, was there. He would probably recognize the sound as another werewolf and tell my mother to stay inside.

I hid behind the shed in case she looked out the window and let out a loud howl that frightened a nearby squirrel. He chattered and ran up a tree. I resisted the urge to chase him, even though I was hungry again. My wolf appetite was insatiable. Or maybe I just needed to catch bigger game than rabbits and opossums. I hadn't figured out how to sneak up on a deer yet.

Antsy, I let out a few more howls till I heard the screen door squeak open. I peeked my head around the corner of the shed and saw my father moving slowly towards me, with my brother a few paces behind him. Thankfully, neither one of them had a shotgun in their hands.

My father called out quietly but sternly, "Who are you? What do you want? Shift and show yourself."

I tried broadcasting my thoughts to him like I did to Nikko, but he didn't act like he could hear me. I guess he had to be in wolf form for that to work. I let out one more plaintive cry then dropped to my belly and crawled out from behind the shed so they'd know I meant them no harm. Still, they moved towards me cautiously, scanning the area around me.

When they got close enough to see that no one else was hiding behind the shed to attack them, my father yanked off his shirt, dropped his pants, and morphed in a sudden explosion of fur and contorting bone. My brother followed right after him. They stood before me, a large, black and silver wolf and a smaller brown one. I'd seen them shift with my own eyes, but I still couldn't believe they were my father and brother.

"Daddy, it's Luna!" I cried out in my mind, in case they intended to attack me. I didn't know anything about wolf protocol, but I assumed they'd consider a strange wolf on their property who wouldn't shift a threat. Fear bristled the fur on the nape of my neck.

My father padded closer, sniffing the air. Did I smell anything like my human self? My brother moved closer, too. They could probably smell Nikko on me and would think it was a trick of the enemy.

But my father must've smelled something familiar, because he ran his snout up and down my flank then looked me in the eyes. "Luna? What? How? Is it really you?"

"It's me, Daddy. Please help me," I whimpered.

Zander paced back and forth several feet behind my father, chuffing and whining. "No way, no freakin' way. This cannot be possible."

"Smell her, Zander. It's your sister."

Zander came close enough to get a good whiff then stiffened and stared at me. "Holy shit. She smells like Nikko."

"Watch your language, son." My dad scowled at him but didn't address the elephant in the room. I guess the wolf was a big enough issue.

To me, he said softly, "Tell us what happened, Luna."

I whined and looked at my brother. It was humiliating enough to tell my father about my first sexual experience, I didn't want to tell my little brother, too. Especially considering the way he was looking at me in disgust.

My father sat down next to me. "This is pack business. We need to know the truth."

I sighed and gave the shortest version possible, fudging the truth just a little. "I'd been feeling kind of... funny for the last few days, and I was at the fall festival. Nikko was there, and we... I couldn't control myself; it was like I was out of my mind!"

Dad nodded. "You're in heat. I can smell it on you."

I hung my head, embarrassed and ashamed. I didn't deserve his understanding. I should've controlled myself, or at least found someone else to have sex with besides the enemy.

"That was when I changed, and Nikko did, too. He bit me and..." I couldn't bring myself to admit the rest of it, but I was pretty sure they both knew what had happened.

"I didn't know what he was doing. I was so freaked out, scared. I knocked him off me and ran away, but it was too late. He caught up to me and told me about you and Zander and the two packs, and how he had... claimed me."

Zander howled, but Dad just laid his head on top of mine. "It's alright, Luna. It's not your fault."

Zander bellowed, "Yes it is her fault! You told her to stay away from Nikko. I told her to stay away from Nikko. But what does she do the minute we're gone? She goes and fuc—"

"Enough!" Dad snapped at Zander, growling. "She's in estrus. The urge is too powerful to resist."

"She could've mated with any wolf in our pack! But

no, she had to choose him." Zander snarled and stalked back and forth, glaring at me.

"She had no idea what she was getting into." Dad's face wrinkled with guilt, making me feel even worse. It was my fault. I should've listened to him.

"But Nikko did. He was all up on her the minute she walked into school the other day. I should've kicked his ass then," Zander grumbled.

Dad growled at him. "And risked starting a pack war? That would've been just as bad."

Guilt weighed heavy on me, and I hung my head. "There may be one, anyway. Nikko said if I didn't join his pack and become his mate, his father would come after me."

Zander let out a loud howl, but Dad bit his throat to shush him then looked around to make sure none of our neighbors had poked their heads out to see what kind of animal had made the sound. When he was sure the coast was clear, he gave Zander another warning growl and turned back to me.

"You don't need to worry about that, Luna. I'll take care of things from here. I'm sorry you had to go through all of this alone. Believe me, if I'd had any inkling that you were going to shift, I'd have prepared you."

His words softened the anxiety coiled inside me. I considered myself strong and independent, but this was all too much for me. I was still just a teenage girl, even if I was a powerful werewolf.

"Nikko told me there are no other female wolves."

"He's right. You're very special." Dad nuzzled me under my chin. I'd never gotten so much attention from him. It was kind of nice.

"I don't feel special; I feel like a freak." Zander's look told me he felt the same way about me.

Dad got up and nudged me to do the same. "Let's get you inside. Your mother will be relieved to see you. She said you texted her that you were spending the weekend at Macy's, but she was worried because you haven't been returning her texts."

"Nikko sent the first text. I can't work the phone with these paws, and I don't know how to shift back. That's why I've been hiding in the woods all weekend." I glanced up at the moon that still looked full and bright. How much did it have to wane before it lost its hold on me?

"I'll help you tonight and teach you how later. Shift," he commanded, his voice stronger, more powerful than I'd ever heard it. The word echoed through me like a hypnotist's command, forcing my body to obey.

My bones contorted with another series of painful cracks, my body squeezing in on itself till I was human size again. Flesh covered my fur, wrapping tight around me like a bandage. I thought I would feel relieved, but instead, I felt strange, like I was wearing an ill-fitting costume. Being human didn't feel right anymore.

Suddenly, I realized I was standing naked in front of my father and brother. I yelped and wrapped my arms around my body. Dad grabbed his shirt off the ground and tossed it to me. I quickly turned around and pulled it over my head. It was just a tee shirt, but since he was a lot bigger than me, it covered all the important parts. When I turned back around, they'd shifted, too, and put their pants back on.

We went inside, and I headed to my room, flexing my arms and legs experimentally, rediscovering my human form. But before I got there, I overheard my brother talking to my father in the kitchen. I couldn't resist sneaking back down the hall to listen. If I pressed my back to the wall, I could see and hear them, but they couldn't see me. It was a trick my brother and I had perfected over the years, eavesdropping on our parents.

"What the hell, Dad? How is she a wolf?" Zander whispered.

Dad pulled a bottle of whiskey down from the cupboard above the fridge and poured himself a shot in a glass tumbler, downing it in one gulp. I'd never seen him drink before.

"The only thing I can guess is that your mother must have wolf blood in her birth family. But since she was adopted, she doesn't know anything about them. That could help explain why Bardolf and I were both so drawn to her as pups."

Zander pulled a chair away from the table with a squeak and sat down. "Bardolf wanted Mom?"

Dad took the bottle of whiskey and his empty glass and sat down beside him, carefully lifting the chair so it wouldn't make noise instead of dragging it. "But she chose me, even though he was in line to be alpha. He never got over it, and he tried to make our lives miserable. That was part of the reason I left. He was cruel and heartless, and when he got power, he was even worse."

"Do you think he'll try to force Luna to join his pack?"

"Most definitely. He'll consider it the perfect revenge, stealing my daughter, my firstborn." Dad poured another shot and drank it with shaking hands then immediately poured a third one. Guilt burned my throat like I was the one drinking.

"Firstborn—you mean to say she's…"

Dad nodded. "She's a wolf; that's all that matters."

"Holy shit!" My brother grabbed my dad's drink and tossed it back. My father didn't say a word about the foul language or the drinking.

What were they talking about? It was obviously a huge deal. It involved me, so I wanted to know about it. I stomped out to the kitchen and yanked out a chair, sitting down between them.

"What are you saying about me?"

Zander sneered at me. "Just stay out of it, Luna. You've caused enough trouble as it is. Let us handle it."

"I don't need you to handle it for me. I got myself into this mess, I can get myself out. Just tell me what I need to do."

Dad raised an eyebrow at Zander. "She's got the personality for it, that's for sure."

"No way! Just because she's bossy doesn't mean she's meant to be…" Zander flashed me a glare.

"Be what?" I glared back at him.

"Nothing. Never mind."

"Zander, she's an important part of this pack now; she deserves to know." Dad turned to me. "The firstborn wolf of an alpha is in line to be the next alpha."

"You mean me? I'm supposed to be the alpha? But I don't know anything about the pack!"

"Exactly! It's ridiculous." Zander pounded his fist on the table, shaking it.

Dad scowled at him and put a hand over his fist. "Don't wake your mother."

I smirked at him. "I take it you thought you were next in line."

Zander bared his teeth at me and let out a low growl. I couldn't resist growling back at him. No wonder we'd always been in a pissing match with each other.

"No fighting! We have bigger concerns right now. Besides, I don't plan to die any time soon. Both of you go to bed. I'll come up with a plan, and we'll discuss it in the morning." My father shooed us away with a look we didn't dare defy.

As much as I wanted to solve this problem I'd created, I had no idea how to, so I was grateful that my father seemed confident. But I couldn't help but remember the way his hands shook as he poured the whiskey. I had a feeling there was no good solution.

CHAPTER 10

NIKKO

I STARED AT THE CLOCK THE WHOLE NIGHT, WATCHING THE minutes tick past like a countdown timer on a bomb, waiting for my dad to get home. They went by torturously slow yet way too fast at the same time. When the door slammed, it felt like my heart exploded.

He stomped into the living room, naked, smelling like wolf and forest, his pulse pounding from the thrill of the hunt. His eyes immediately zeroed in on me and narrowed.

"Where's the girl?"

I cowered in the corner of the leather sectional, wishing I could hide behind it, but I had to act confident, like I had a plan, even though I didn't. "This is all so new to her. She needs a little more time to adjust to the idea."

Dad sneered at me. "I should've known you couldn't deal with this on your own. I thought you'd grown some balls when you claimed her, but no, you're still just a pathetic, little pup, letting your mate boss you around.

You're nowhere near ready to be alpha. I ought to challenge you for her and claim her as my own."

"What? No!" I jumped up in horror. He wouldn't really do something like that, would he? But I knew immediately that he would.

"Then go get her and bring her back here. I'll come with you to make sure you don't fail again." He stalked off to get dressed.

I rushed after him, desperate to stall. "But it's Monday. I have school."

He spun around and growled at me. "This is more important than school! The longer you let this go on, the weaker you look. She's already shown you up once."

A few minutes later, he emerged from his bedroom, dressed in jeans and a tight, black tee shirt that showed off his massive physique. He hadn't showered, but that only made him seem more intimidating. He stomped towards the back door and grabbed the keys off the counter. "Let's go."

As I followed him, I caught a glimpse of myself in the mirror my mom used to check her makeup in before she left the house. Would things be different if she was still around? Would my dad be less heartless, less demanding? I looked weak and haggard compared to him in rumpled, day-old clothes with dark circles under my eyes from staying up all night, worrying. I dragged myself out to his mud-covered truck and climbed in. The heavy door closed on me with an ominous thud.

He'd been up all night, too, hunting, but he looked full of dangerous energy, his eyes wide and wild. He revved the truck, spraying dirt and gravel as he spun it around and took off, fishtailing. I clenched the door handle as he bounced down the pitted drive like it was a superhighway.

"You're just going to drive into their territory?" As bad as that sounded, it was better than having this confrontation at school. But classes didn't start for a couple more hours, so Luna hadn't left yet, if she was going to school at all. Maybe she was still in the woods, unable to shift back. Or maybe she got smart and ran away. The thought of that tore a hole in my chest, though. As much as I hated to hurt her by demanding she come with us, my wolf clamored for his mate.

"They have no territory. Everything within a hundred miles of here belongs to me and our pack. They're the ones squatting on our land. We should've run them off years ago."

He careened through town like he was begging for a ticket. I wouldn't have minded the distraction, but that would've only made him madder. There was no point delaying the inevitable. I didn't even have Luna's number so I could warn her. Of course, my dad probably would've tossed my phone out the window if I had tried.

The Ammons lived in an old, ranch-style house on the outskirts of town on a dead end street surrounded by a small, wooded area. Still, they didn't have near the privacy that we had on our land. When Dad pulled into their driveway, Lupin Ammon immediately came out the front door.

To his credit, he didn't visibly react, although he looked like he was already wound tight, with his fists and jaw clenched. Zander and Luna followed behind him. Their curious looks hardened into scowls when my dad got out, slammed his door, and stalked towards them.

That close to each other, the height and weight disparity between the two alphas was painfully obvious.

I jumped out of the passenger side and hurried over to them, getting between them. This was my fight, after all. Luna had showered, and the sunrise glimmered off her damp hair and warmed her bare face in a soft glow. A breeze blew her scent towards me, overwhelming me with lust and the need to protect her.

I wanted to rush towards her and take her in my arms, kiss her, touch her. But she and her brother both turned their scowls towards me. Lupin stayed straight-faced. He kept his mouth shut, smart enough not to provoke my dad by complaining about him coming onto his property. He obviously knew why we were there.

Luna's mother peeked her head out the door, giving me a glimpse of what Luna would look like in the future. Softer, curvier, more mature, but still beautiful. "Lupin, what's going on?"

My father sucked in a loud breath at the sight of her. She flicked her pale blue eyes towards him, and they widened as her mouth dropped open. "Bardolf?"

"He's here to talk to me, Donna. Go inside," Lupin said firmly. She stared at us for a moment longer then ducked back into the house.

"You have something that belongs to my son." Dad's voice was as hard and gravelly as stone.

Zander sneered between me and my dad and started to push past his. "Can't he stand up for himself? He needs his daddy to fight his battles?"

"Zander!" Lupin put out a hand to hold him back.

My father smirked at Zander but didn't take the bait. "That's why he's here, to fight for what's his. Luna belongs to him. If she wants her freedom, she'll need to challenge him for it."

"What?" Everyone but my father gasped out the same thing.

What was my father thinking? I couldn't fight my own mate! If I threw the fight, I'd never live down the shame. Plus, I'd lose my mate, and being apart from her for just a few days had been torture. Death was the only thing that broke the mate bond, but I sure as hell wasn't going to kill her.

She had to be feeling some of the same pull towards me because of the bond. Why couldn't she see that this was a no-win situation and accept her fate? I'd do everything I could to make her happy.

Lupin pushed his daughter behind him. "That's absurd. Luna can't fight. She's an untrained pup. And she's still in heat. That gives your son an unfair advantage."

"Fine. Then you can fight in her place. But you'll fight me instead." Dad stuck his face in Lupin's and snapped his teeth, proving just how ruthless he was. Luna would never want to submit to him, and I didn't blame her.

"No!" Luna grabbed her father's arm. "I'll—"

"Quiet!" Lupin barked at her. She jolted and dropped her hand.

He swallowed hard and stared down my father for a long moment. Eventually, he said, "I've just returned from a hunt and haven't slept. Give me a day to recover."

"Fine. We'll meet this time tomorrow at the old mill—neutral territory."

He'd never admit it, but my father was probably exhausted, too. That was the only reason I could think of why he would agree to the delay. Of course, given his physical advantage, he could probably still take down Lupin without a problem.

He stalked back to the truck and jumped in, but I lingered for a moment, staring at Luna, begging for her forgiveness. Her father was going to die tomorrow, at my father's hand. Then she'd be forced to join my pack and mate with me. She'd hate me forever.

I could see no other outcome unless she decided to come voluntarily. But the way she was looking at me, I knew that wasn't going to happen. I doubted her father would even let her. He'd sacrifice himself trying to prevent the inevitable.

I knew my father would never back down from a challenge and risk losing face, but there had to be something I could do to stop this. An idea came to me, but it was insane. It would cost me everything, and I wasn't sure it would even work. But it might be the only way to save Luna and her father.

CHAPTER 11

LUNA

THE MINUTE BARDOLF'S TRUCK DROVE AWAY, I GRABBED MY father, digging my nails into his arms. "Daddy, I don't want you to fight him. I'll do what they want."

He laid his hands on my arms gently. "No, Luna. I appreciate your willingness, but I won't let you do that. You saw what that man is like. I don't want you to live under his rule or be bound to his son."

He turned to go inside, but I grabbed his arm and pulled him back. No way was this conversation over. "Did you see him? He's enormous! If you try to fight him, he'll kill you, and they'll take me, anyway. I'd rather go voluntarily than have you die trying to protect me."

His face rumpled. He knew it was the truth. He looked ten years older than he did a few days ago, his skin sallow and creased with worry. Were those gray hairs sprouting from his temples?

"I wouldn't be able to live with myself if I gave you up without a fight. I fought Bardolf for your mother and won, I fought him for my freedom and won, so don't count this old dog out."

He stroked my cheek, smiling sadly, then turned and went inside. I didn't try to argue with him again. I could tell it was a matter of pride for him. Why did men have to be so stubborn? But I was just as stubborn as he was, and I wasn't going to give up easily, either.

Zander glared at me and shook his head once Dad was gone. "You just killed our father, Luna. Good job."

"I don't need a lecture, Zander."

He got up in my face and snarled. "Yes, you do! If you'd done what we told you to, none of this would've happened. You never disobey your alpha."

I growled back at him through gritted teeth. "Well, I'm sorry, but I didn't know I had one! I didn't know anything about this. I just thought it was a Montague and Capulet sort of thing. I didn't know I was starting a werewolf pack war. I'm not going to let Dad fight. I'll fix this."

I yanked open the door and headed for my room, but Zander followed me in, closing my bedroom door behind us. "How? By submitting to Nikko's claim? You can't do that. That'll kill him, too."

"Maybe so, but at least it'll be slowly." I grabbed a large duffel bag out of the back of my closet.

Zander grabbed the bag away from me. "Luna, no! It'll undermine his authority as alpha and dishonor our pack."

"Who cares about the pack? All I care about is Dad!" Hangers clattered to the floor as I yanked some clothes out of the closet, rolled them up, and stuck them in my bag.

Zander threw them all out again, tossing them onto my bed. "Dad does, and so do I! And everyone else in it."

"Well, what happens to the pack if Dad dies tomorrow?"

Zander ducked his head. "Nikko claims you, and I become the new alpha."

"That's what you want, isn't it?" I sneered. But the look on his face made me instantly regret it.

His voice quivered. "You know that's not true."

"What do you suggest I do, then?"

He looked down at my duffel then back up at me, clenching his jaw.

"Just say it, Zander."

He ran a hand over my duffel. "If you ran away, there would be nothing for them to fight over."

I stared at him for a moment then down at my duffel. I'd dismissed the idea before, but I'd do it if it meant sparing my dad. I'd always intended to go off and make my own life after I finished school, anyway. I might never be able to come back here, but I could find ways to get messages to my family so they'd know I was safe. Maybe eventually I'd learn to control my wolf, and I could forget all about werewolves and pack wars and live a normal life.

"Ok, I'll do it." My trembling voice belied my confidence.

Zander gave me a pained look. "I'm sorry, Luna. As much as we fight, you know I love you. If there was any other way..."

I grabbed him and yanked him to me, wrapping my arms around him and rubbing his fuzzy head. As big as he'd gotten lately, he was still my little brother, and I loved the twerp. He needed a father more than he needed a sister, though. Especially if he had a pack of werewolves for enemies.

When my tears started to drip down his back, I wiped my eyes and pushed him away. His were moist, too. "I need to pack. Go get ready for school, and I'll drop you off on my way."

He winced. "You're leaving right now?"

"Might as well get a head start so I can be far away before they realize I'm gone."

He picked up the world atlas off my desk and flipped through the dog-eared pages. "Where are you going to go?"

I took the book from him and pulled a stack of bills out from the center—all the money I'd been saving for years to fund my future adventures. That was how I needed to view this, as the start of my first adventure, and not as the end of the life I knew. "I don't know. But maybe it's better if you don't know, either."

Zander watched as I counted the cash. When I'd been saving it, it seemed like a lot, but it would probably only last me a few weeks.

"How much money do you have? Dad can probably give you some. Are you going to tell him?"

I shoved it in my pocket. "Not if you think he'll try to stop me."

"He won't like it, but I think he'll see it's the best solution. You're doing the right thing."

I nodded and shoved him towards the door. I felt more tears welling up. When he left, I sniffed them back. Now wasn't the time to feel sorry for myself. I needed to be brave and confident, and letting myself cry would only make me feel weak.

I filled my duffel bag with as much as I could pack in, but there was no room for anything impractical like the medals and trophies I was so proud of or even my basketball. I wouldn't have time for games, anyway. It would take all my energy just to survive.

Still, I ran my fingers longingly over the row of paperback books on the shelf above my desk. Most of them I'd collected as a kid and hadn't read in years, not since I got a cell phone, but I hated to leave them behind.

I probably shouldn't take the phone with me, either. Would Nikko's pack go so far as to track down my cell phone signal? I needed to ask my father about that, find out how "off the grid" I needed to be.

When I'd packed everything I needed, I left my bag on my bed and went to look for my father. I found him in his bedroom, sitting on his bed, holding a family photo taken a few years ago when I still looked like a kid. I sat down next to him and put my head on his shoulder, wishing I could go back in time. He wrapped an arm around me and pressed his chin to the top of my head. I felt him suck in a shaky breath.

"Dad, I'm going to leave town."

He pulled away so he could look at me. "What? No. I can't ask that of you."

"You're not. This is what I want to do. I think it's the best thing for everybody. Nobody will have to fight, and I won't have to join Nikko's pack. I'm not a little kid anymore. I can take care of myself."

He stared at me for a long moment, a million emotions flashing through his storm cloud eyes. His brows knit together, wrinkling his forehead, and he pressed his lips together in a hard line. Eventually, he nodded.

"I've heard of a place, a sanctuary of sorts, for people

like us. It'll be a safe place for you to learn to control your wolf."

His words blew a puff of hope into my chest. Maybe I didn't have to be all alone. "Where is it?"

"I don't know the exact location, but I'll show you where I think it is." He got up and went over to his bookcase then pulled out an old map book, the pages yellowed and brittle. He opened it up and pointed to a mountainous area a few hundred miles south.

He ran his finger down a series of roads leading from here to there. "You can take the highway to here, but then you'll need to look for a pass through the mountains. I don't know what to tell you to look for, but hopefully you'll know it when you see it. You might have to shift and go on foot to get through these mountains."

"I don't know how to make myself shift, or how to shift back."

He tore the page out of the map and handed it to me. "I'm going to send Zander with you. He can teach you what you need to know."

"What? Dad, no."

"He can protect you."

"Dad, he's younger than me. He's still a kid."

He smirked. "Okay, so you can protect each other."

I couldn't let Dad lose both his kids in one day, and I couldn't steal Zander's life from him. I didn't want to spend my last few minutes with my dad arguing with him, though. "I'll send him back after I get there and get settled in."

"Fair enough."

Dad pulled his wallet out of his back pocket and

handed me all the cash in it—a couple hundred dollars. "I'll go to the bank and get some more."

I pulled out my own wad and showed it to him. "It's okay, I've got some. I was thinking I should leave as soon as possible."

He gulped and nodded, his eyes dampening. "Say goodbye to your mother, but don't tell her anything. I'll figure out something to tell her later. I'll talk to Zander while you do."

I nodded then threw myself at him, burying my face in his chest, memorizing the musky scent of him and the feel of his soft, worn flannel shirt. He ran his hands down my hair, stroking my back. "I'm so sorry, Daddy. I'll miss you."

"I'm sorry, too, sweetheart. Hopefully someday it will be safe for you to come home again," he murmured into my hair.

A lot of things would need to change for that to happen, but there was always a chance. I buried that nugget of hope deep in my heart.

I dropped my bag by the front door then headed down the hall to find my mom while Dad went to Zander's room. I had a feeling that conversation would be rough, so I was glad Dad was tackling it. But saying goodbye to my mother, without letting her know it might be the last time she'd ever see me, was going to be even harder.

I found her in the kitchen, as usual, humming to herself as she washed the breakfast dishes. In that moment, everything was perfect in her world. There were no werewolves, no pack wars, no runaway daughters. I wished she could stay in that bubble forever. But in a few hours, it would burst completely. I had no idea how my dad would explain my disappearance, but no matter what he said, she wouldn't understand.

I grabbed her from behind and yelled, "boo!" on the pretense of scaring her, but I really just wanted an excuse to hug her one last time. She yelped and dropped a dish into the sink, splashing herself with soapy water.

She whirled around and gaped at me. "Luna! What was that for?"

"Sorry, Mom. Couldn't resist." I grinned at her, hoping she couldn't see the pain behind my smile, and wiped the suds off her cheek.

She smiled back then gave me a peck on the nose. "Have a good day at school, dear."

There was so much I wanted to say to her, but she might've gotten suspicious if I'd gone all mushy on her. Instead, all I said was, "Love you, Mom."

Her face melted. "Love you too, sweetie."

I forced another smile then quickly turned around before she could see the tears welling up in my eyes. Zander came out into the kitchen then, presumably to say his own goodbyes. I glanced at him then headed for the door. "I'll be in the truck."

I wiped my cheeks and blinked away the moisture in my eyes while I waited for Zander. If I let myself cry, I knew I wouldn't be able to stop. I'd wait till I was all alone to mourn. Zander climbed in a few minutes later, carrying a backpack full to bursting.

I didn't say anything for the first few minutes of the drive. I was too busy debating with myself about what to do with Zander. Should I take him with me, or leave him behind?

It would be nice to have someone with me, especially

someone who could fill me in on all this wolf stuff. Maybe I could do like I told Dad and let Zander help me find the place then send him home. But Mom would be doubly upset if we both took off, and how would Zander explain it to her when he got back? Plus, what if Nikko's pack started a fight when they learned I'd run off? Taking Zander with me would keep him safe, but it would leave Dad with less protection.

Zander seemed to sense my need for quiet so I could think, or maybe he needed it, too. Was he angry that Dad wanted him to go with me or eager for the adventure? Either way, he didn't speak till I turned into the school parking lot. "What are you doing? Dad told me to go with you."

"I know, but I left my favorite jacket in my locker. Would you go get it for me? I don't want to risk seeing Nikko again." I gave him my most innocent, terrified look.

He frowned at me but then opened his door. "Okay. What's your locker combination?"

I rattled it off then told him I'd meet him by the back doors where we were less likely to be seen leaving. As soon as he walked inside, I drove off. I did pull around to the back, but only to toss his book bag onto the sidewalk where he'd find it when he came out to look for me. I'd caused enough trouble for my family, I had to fix this on my own.

CHAPTER 12

NIKKO

Dᴀᴅ sᴘᴇᴅ ᴀᴡᴀʏ ꜰʀᴏᴍ Lᴜɴᴀ's ʜᴏᴜsᴇ, ʀᴇᴠᴠᴇᴅ ᴜᴘ ᴏɴ testosterone and adrenaline, the scent of his emotions thick in the enclosed space. He thrived on this kind of thing, the more intense and dangerous the better. Meanwhile, I felt sick to my stomach, and my body was trembling like I had the flu. Did I have the guts to do what I needed to do to save Luna and her father?

I thought Dad would be mad that he had to fight my battle, but instead, he seemed stoked by the outcome. His lips curled in a malicious grin. "This is going to work out perfect. Lupin will never be able to win a fight against me. I'll take him down, you'll claim Luna, then his pack will have no choice but to submit to me."

I gawked at him, my mouth hanging open wide enough to catch flies. "You're going to try to take over his pack?"

"It's my pack, not his! It always has been. I didn't have the power to stop him back when he and his followers first left the pack, but now I'm stronger and I have every advantage. It's time to take back what's mine." He pounded his hands against the steering wheel, punctuating each declaration.

It was bad enough that he wanted to force Luna to mate with me and join our pack, but killing her father and taking over their pack was going too far. I had to stop him. I wasn't strong enough to fight him, but maybe I was smart enough foil his plans.

I stayed quiet the rest of the drive. He didn't notice, he was too caught up in his fantasies of domination. When we got home, I mumbled that I was going to get ready for school than headed off to my room.

We had a log home, but it was no cabin. When my mom was alive, she decorated the huge house with high-end, rustic style furniture, and Dad had outfitted it with every modern luxury. But I didn't appreciate any of it. When Mom died, all the warmth and homeyness went out of the place.

When I was home, I rarely left my room. That small corner of the house was my haven, the only place I could hide from the reality of my life. There, I could forget about my dead mom, my power hungry dad, the struggles of being a werewolf, and my glaring unsuitability as the next alpha. We had money, power, and prestige, but I wouldn't miss much about my life here. But I would miss the comfort of this space and the security of my place in our pack.

When I walked in, the wood walls, plaid curtains, and soft, navy rug cocooned me, tempting me to hole up inside and hide from my problems. I forced myself to pull a bag from my closet and toss in as much as I could fit. I'd withdraw all the money from my account and buy whatever else I needed. I had plenty of money; too bad I couldn't buy my way out of this mess. But Luna didn't seem like the type who'd take a bribe, and neither did her father.

I could hear Dad clanking weights in the gym, so I slung my heavy bag over my shoulder and headed for the front door without looking back, calling out to him as I left, "I'm leaving for school."

I didn't bother waiting for a response. I doubted there'd be one, any way. He was focused on his own schemes. I hated him sometimes, but he was my father, and the only family I had. I wished we could have a real goodbye, but he'd be suspicious if I acted any different than normal.

My body felt so heavy, it took all my strength to carry my bag. With a grunt, I heaved it into the passenger seat of my SUV then climbed in. I took one last long, lingering look at the place I'd called home my whole life before starting the car. Would I ever come back there and claim my place as alpha? I had no idea what the future held.

When I got to the road, I stopped for a long moment, debating which way to go. I had no plan, no destination in mind. All I knew was I had to leave.

Out of habit, I turned towards town. I wished I could see my friends again; I hated losing them. But I couldn't risk telling them what I was doing. I needed to be far away before my dad found out I was leaving. I slowed down when I got to the school, but I didn't pull in. I kept driving, past the main entrance, silently saying goodbye.

A gray truck pulled out of the back entrance a couple cars in front of me. It only took me a second to recognize it. Luna. Why was she leaving? Maybe she was taking the day off school to prepare herself for what was to come. She had to know what was bound to happen tomorrow. Maybe I should tell her what I was planning, let her know I was doing the only thing I knew to save her.

She drove past the main section of town, past the road that led to her house. Where was she going? My curiosity kept me following her, even when the cars in between us turned off. She didn't seem to notice me behind her, though. She was probably too distracted by her own worries.

But then she put on her blinker and slowed down to turn into a gas station. Was she still unaware of me, or did she want me to stop, too? Either way, I wasn't going to miss the opportunity. If nothing else, I wanted to see her one last time.

She pulled in next to a gas pump, got out, and opened the flap to the gas tank on her truck then stuck in the nozzle. She didn't even look up when I parked on the side of the building and walked over to her. "Luna?"

She jumped and whirled around, a guilty, frightened look on her face. "Nikko! What are you doing?"

"I saw you pull out of the school. I wanted to talk to you." Just being next to her again soothed some of my anxiety, but she obviously didn't feel the same way.

Her eyes flicked nervously between the gas tank behind her and the door of her truck, like she wanted to escape, but I was in between them. I glanced in her truck and saw a large duffel on the seat, packed to the seams. It looked a lot like the one in my own vehicle.

"Leave me alone, Nikko. I don't want anything to do with you." She grabbed the gas nozzle and squeezed hard like she was trying to speed it up. Her hands shook, rattling the metal.

My wolf roared to life inside me, demanding I claim what was mine. "Where are you going?"

"It's none of your business." She jerked the nozzle out of her tank. Gas flung out, splashing her and the side of the truck. The sharp, acrid scent filled the space around us. But it wasn't enough to overpower the scent of her.

She must've seen the look of desire in my eyes, because her heart rate sped up, and she started breathing heavy, sucking in the fumes. I put my hand on hers, hoping to calm her down, but she yanked hers away like my touch disgusted her, even though a few days ago she couldn't get enough of me.

All of a sudden, I couldn't fathom the thought of giving her up. I'd claimed her, and she was mine, whether she liked it or not. All she had to do was submit to me, and everything would be fine.

I grabbed her wrist tight enough that she yelped. "I won't let you run away, Luna. Your dad's gonna die tomorrow, and my dad is going to take over your pack. But if you give in and mate with me, that doesn't have to happen."

She sneered at me, and she might as well have been shooting arrows into me with her eyes. "Do you really want a mate who doesn't want to be with you? None of that has to happen if you give up your stupid claim on me."

I wanted her more than anything. How could she not feel at least a little bit of that?Maybe because I was being a jerk, bossing her around and demanding she give up everything she loved.

I was acting just like my dad, and I hated when he treated me that way. She was right; I didn't want a mate who hated me and was only with me out of obligation. I had to find a way to make Luna want to be with me.

I softened my voice and my grip on her wrist. "It's not that simple. My dad won't let me do that. You saw what he's like."

"Yeah, he's an ass, just like you."

"I'm not like him, Luna, I swear. I'm so sorry about all of this. I can't change what happened, but I would if I could. I have an idea, though. Let me go with you, wherever you're going. He can't make me claim you if neither one of us is here. I won't force you to mate with me, I promise."

I could see her determination wavering as she considered my offer. She had to be scared to be leaving everything she knew and running off on her own. I knew I was. Maybe I could soothe those worries.

"You don't have to be alone, Luna. I'll take care of you. No strings attached."

She stayed silent for a long time, considering her options. I dared to stroke a finger down her cheek. Her soft skin was chilled from the cool air, but I could feel the heat of her pulsing blood seeping through. The skin pinked under my touch. Maybe she did feel some of the same attraction.

But then her face hardened, and she pulled away from me. "You wouldn't run away from home, leave your pack, and give up your alpha status to protect me and my dad without expecting something. What do you want?"

"I know I screwed up your life. I just want to make it up to you. Will you give me a chance?"

Maybe it was the mate bond, or her fear of going off on her own, or maybe my sincerity shone through, but, whatever the reason, by some miracle she gave a tiny nod. I resisted the urge to grab her and hug her. Instead, I took her hand and tugged her towards my SUV. "Come on. My vehicle's nicer."

But she dug in her heels and yanked her hand out of mine. "No way. You can come with me, but I call the shots. We're taking my truck, and I'm driving."

I didn't care, as long as we were together. "Yes, ma'am."

I hurried over to my SUV and grabbed my bag off the seat then hustled back over to her truck before she could change her mind and drive off without me. I opened the passenger door to her truck, grabbed her bag, chucked both in the back, then climbed in beside her.

She raised an eyebrow at me. "Why do you have a bag?"

I didn't want to admit that I was planning to leave in hopes that my Dad would drop the fight over her if I wasn't there to claim her. She might think that was a good alternative to us running off together. But considering how eager my dad was about the opportunity to fight Lupin, I doubted my absence would change his plan, anyway. But her absence would change Lupin's mind. This was better for everyone.

I made up an excuse on the fly. "It's just some clothes I keep with me in case I shift and tear mine."

"Convenient." She smirked, and I wasn't sure she believed my cover story, but she didn't question it. Instead, she started the truck, releasing a blast of air from the vents that swirled her scent around, intoxicating me. I looked at my groin and commanded it to behave. It was going to be a long trip with no guarantees. I might never be able to win over Luna. But at least I had a shot.

"So, where are we going?"

CHAPTER 13

LUNA

I stared at Nikko, sitting next to me in my truck, looking gorgeous, smelling incredible, and obviously addling my brain. What was I thinking letting him come with me? He was the last person I should be running away with.

I had to be careful not to let my guard down around him. I still didn't trust him. But as worried as I was that this was some kind of a setup, having him there eased my anxiety in a way I couldn't explain.

"I'm not telling you anything. If you want to come, be quiet and do what I say. And give me your cell phone." I held out a hand towards him.

"What?"

"Your cell phone. I don't want you calling your dad or anyone else in your pack and telling them where I am."

"Luna, I'm not trying to trick you. You can trust me."

"No, I can't. Trust is earned." I shoved my hand towards him again.

He sighed but pulled out his cell phone and laid it on

my palm. "How can I ever earn your trust if you don't give me a chance to prove I'm trustworthy?"

"Not my problem." I tapped the phone screen awake to see if there were any nefarious messages immediately visible, but all I got was the lock screen.

"The passcode is 0000," he mumbled, crossing his arms over his chest.

I rolled my eyes at him and tapped in the code. A quick glance didn't reveal anything worrisome, so I went to the settings, turned off everything that might broadcast our location, then shut down the phone and stuck it in my pocket.

Satisfied that I was safe, at least temporarily, I pulled out of the gas station and headed for the highway. Nikko stayed silent, making the truck seem too quiet, so I turned up the radio. I curled my lip at the pop song that was playing and searched for a different station, stopping when I heard my favorite song. Nikko glanced curiously at me.

"Is this okay?"

"Yeah, yeah. It's great. I love this song."

Now it was my turn to look at him. Did we actually have something in common? "Me too."

I sang a few words, and he joined me. We sang together for several lines, but his voice was so compelling, I let mine fade away so I could listen to him. After a few lines, he stopped, too.

"Don't stop; it's nice. You have a good voice."

He scoffed at me and shook his head. "You really think so?"

"I'm serious! Keep going."

"Only if you sing with me."

"Okay." I shrugged and started singing again. He joined me, and I lowered my voice just enough that he could still hear me, but I could hear him better.

We sang several more songs together till my voice got scratchy. I stopped, but Nikko serenaded me a bit longer. They were just words to a love song, but the way he looked at me as he sang them made me think he meant them.

He couldn't love me; he barely knew me. And I certainly couldn't love him, especially after what he did to me. So why did I have these feelings every time he was around? Why had I let him come with me?

He implied before that we had some kind of bond since we had mated. I didn't want to accept that, but how else could I explain why I felt drawn to him even though the logical thing would be to run as far away from him as possible? Instead, I was dragging him along with me. It was crazy. I should kick him out right now.

But instead, I started asking him questions like I wanted to get to know him or something.

"When did you learn that you were... a wolf?" It still sounded crazy when I said it.

"My dad told me when I was really young, just after my mom died. I guess it was easier for him than trying to keep it a secret since he's the alpha and has a lot of dealings with the other wolves. It was hard, though, knowing but not being one of them yet. I couldn't wait for my first shift."

"So you like being a wolf?" I couldn't fathom that. Finding out I was a wolf had effectively ruined my whole life.

He shrugged. "It was all I knew. There's a certain sense

of freedom and power that it brings. But there are a lot of expectations, too, at least for me, anyway."

"Like what?"

"Well, I'm next in line to be alpha, so everyone expects me to be the strongest, the best at everything. My dad won't settle for anything less. But I never seem to live up to his expectations. He constantly tells me I'll never be a good alpha."

"That's harsh."

"I don't even want to be alpha, especially not if it means being like him."

All of a sudden, I felt sorry for him. Maybe Nikko wasn't as big of a jerk as I thought. Maybe he was just trying to please his father. After seeing what his dad was like, it was a wonder Nikko wasn't even more of an asshole.

"Was he like that before your mom died?"

He stared at me for a long moment then nodded solemnly. "He killed her. He lost his temper, grabbed her, and shook her. She died in his arms. I watched it happen."

I gasped, and my mouth hung open, unable to form words.

"The medical examiner said she had an aneurysm, said it was a time bomb waiting to go off, but I still blame my dad. If he hadn't shook it loose, who knows how much longer she might've had before it burst on it's own?"

"Oh Nikko, I'm so sorry." On impulse, I reached for his hand and squeezed it. It was cold and shaking even though the heater and our wolf body temperatures had warmed up the cab.

He looked down at our joined hands and swallowed hard. "I've never told anyone that."

I gave him a look that let him know I appreciated him sharing with me, but I stayed quiet so he could tell me more if he wanted to. It seemed like he needed to get it out.

He looked out the window, telling the rest of the story to the passing scenery like I wasn't even there, but his grip on my hand let me know he was glad I was. "After she died, he didn't seem to mourn her or anything. He just threw himself back double time into his duties as alpha. He never talked about her after that. I'm not sure he ever really loved her."

My dad's words to my brother came back to me. Bardolf had wanted my mother, but Dad had won her heart. Maybe Bardolf never did love the woman he eventually married.

"Tell me about your mom." What I really wanted to know was what kind of person would marry Bardolf in the first place, but I didn't want to say that. Nikko understood, though.

He tilted his head and stared out the windshield, lost in memories. "I don't remember much about her, but she was good to me, and I loved her. My grandpa was alpha before she and my dad married. She was his beta's daughter. I guess it was a strategic marriage."

I couldn't help but ask, "But if your Dad was so harsh and unloving, why didn't she leave him?"

He turned and stared at me, capturing me with his intense gaze and squeezing my hand. "Wolves mate for life, Luna. The mate bond is strong. It would've been just as hard for her to leave as it was to stay. Besides, he never would've let her."

I gulped and tore my eyes and hand away from his, my

heart thumping fast and loud in my chest and my palms sweaty. Did that mean our mate bond was just as strong? Maybe it was even more so since we were both wolves. Was that why I felt the way I did every time I was near Nikko, even though my brain told me to stay away from him?

Our contrasting families were proof that marriages based on anything other than love didn't usually work out well. It should've been a reminder to me why I couldn't give in to Nikko's claim. But instead, his story had only made me feel closer to him. Was I destined to live out the same story his mother had, all because of some supernatural wolf bond?

Nikko must've sensed my fears because he rushed to quell them. "I'm not like my dad, Luna. Or, at least, I'm trying not to be. I want to respect your wishes. But the truth is, we're bonded, and we always will be, even if we're not… together."

I wanted to hate him for it; it was all his fault. He never should've claimed me without my permission in the first place. But I still felt drawn towards him. Was that just the bond, or did I really have feelings for him? I guess I'd never know.

It was my turn to stay quiet and contemplate everything I'd learned. He let me think for a while and didn't push me to talk. Eventually, his eyes closed and his head bobbed forward. When his chin hit his chest, he jerked awake and looked at me.

"Sorry, I didn't get much sleep last night."

"Go ahead and nap if you want. We've got a long drive."

He shook his head and smirked. "You really won't tell

me where we're going?"

I trusted him a little bit more now, for some reason, but I still said, "Nope."

Talking about sleep make me remember how little I'd gotten the night before, and a yawn escaped me. His face wrinkled in worry. "You're tired, too. Maybe I should drive so you can nap."

I grinned and shook my head. "Not a chance."

He huffed, took off his jacket, then rolled it up and stuck it between his head and the window. "Fine. Have it your way. But pull over if you get too sleepy. I don't want to die in a car crash."

A few minutes later, he was snoring softly, so I took the opportunity to stare at him. There was no doubt about it, he was definitely nice to look at with that bronze skin and longish, brown hair threaded with shades of gold that matched the flecks in his eyes. I couldn't see them now, but I remembered exactly what they looked like. I'd had a crush on him for years based on his looks alone.

But in the last few days, we'd gone on our first date, had sex, and he'd claimed me as his mate. I'd gotten everything I'd every fantasized about, but it was all so sudden. I barely knew anything about him. Although I'd learned a whole lot in the last few days—things that made me realize why my father warned me to stay away from him, and yet, other things that made me like him even more. I had no idea how to feel about him now.

He dozed till I pulled off the last marked road and onto a gravel path that went in the direction of the mountains my father had pointed out on the map. The bumpy road woke Nikko up, and he jolted upright. He wiped a dribble of drool off his chin, rubbed the sleep from his eyes, then ran a hand through his hair.

"Where are we? Are you lost?"

"Nope."

Nikko gave me a dubious look, but I bumped along as confidently as I could, even though, in truth, I didn't have any idea where to go next. I drove another half an hour, kicking up dust, bouncing over potholes, and basically torturing my poor truck, till the road ended at a red and white wooden crossbar. The path beyond looked totally overgrown, if there was ever a road there at all. I got out and scanned the land around us—large, grassy fields surrounded by tree-covered mountains.

Nikko climbed out and scowled at me over the top of the truck. "Luna. We are definitely lost. Where are you trying to go?"

I supposed there was no reason not to tell him at that point. We were hundreds of miles from home, and even I couldn't pinpoint our location on a map. Plus, I doubted there was any cell signal out this far. No one could track us.

"My father said there's a place out here where people like us can hide. It's not on any map, and he didn't know the exact location, but it's supposed to be out here some-where. He said we might have to go on foot." I waved my hands around the sprawling vista.

Nikko huffed and ran a hand through his hair. "Luna, do you hear yourself? That sounds insane!"

"Yeah, well, I would've said the same thing a few days ago if you'd told me we were both going to turn into werewolves, but that happened, so..." I threw my hands up in the air.

He didn't have a response to that. He just shook his head and blew out his cheeks.

"Look, my father wouldn't send me here unless he thought this place was real. This is where he wanted me to go, so I'm going to do my best to find it. Are you coming or not?"

CHAPTER 14

NIKKO

I SIGHED AND LOOKED AT LUNA, READY TO TREK THROUGH the wilderness, looking for some mythical place. The girl had balls, that was for sure. Probably more than me. But if I wanted her, I was going to have to follow her lead.

"Fine. I'll go with you. I don't think we're going to find anything, though. There's absolutely nothing out here."

Luna grabbed her duffel out of the back of the truck and hoisted it over her shoulder then squeezed past the road block onto the overgrown path. I grabbed mine, too, and hurried after her. Luna had no clue which way to go, and the place wasn't visible, so for lack of a better idea, we followed the old path for a while, thrashing through knee-high overgrowth. It was better than the waist-high grass on either side of us.

Eventually, the trail grew narrower, more rocky, and started to incline as it led towards the mountains ahead. We trudged on until Luna tripped on a rocky outcropping and stumbled, landing with a loud thud and an oomph.

"Are you okay?" I quickly kneeled down to check on her.

"Yeah, I'm fine."

I held out a hand to help her as she scrambled to her feet, but she ignored it, brushing off her dusty pants instead then wiping the sweat off her forehead, smearing it with dirt.

When she tossed her duffel back over her shoulder and started to climb again, I grabbed her arm. "Luna, stop. This is nuts. Look around; there's nothing out here."

She followed my gaze around. There was nothing ahead but mountains. The afternoon sun beat down on us, heating our skin, bathing everything in yellow light, and reminding me the day was already more than half gone. If we didn't find the sanctuary soon, we'd be spending the night out there.

"It's probably hidden on the other side of the mountains. Hopefully, we'll see it once we get to the top." She tilted her head back to see the pinnacle, and my gaze followed hers. It looked miles away, and straight up.

"We can't climb that. Maybe as wolves, but not like this. I think we should turn back." I gestured to our street clothes, sneakers, and obvious lack of any climbing equipment.

"Well, I'm not turning back. But I don't know how to wolf out on demand. Can you teach me?"

"I've never taught anyone how to shift before. I'm not sure I can even explain it."

"Well, how did you learn to shift?"

"My first several shifts were brought on by the moon, like yours. I stayed as a wolf till the moon waned and didn't shift again till the next one. The wolf takes control during the moon. But after a while, you become one with your wolf, and then you can learn to control it. It takes some time."

She dropped her duffel on the ground. "We don't have time. I have to figure this out now. What do you do, just think wolfy thoughts?"

I chuckled and shook my head. "Something like that. Close your eyes."

She raised an eyebrow and stared at me for a moment like she wasn't quite sure she could trust me before eventually crossing her arms and dropping her lids. "Okay, now what."

"Now, try to feel your wolf inside you."

Her eyes popped open and her upper lip curled. "What the heck does that mean? What does my wolf feel like?"

"The day you first shifted, did you feel any differently than normal?"

"Yeah."

"How did you feel?"

She blushed, immediately rousing my curiosity, but pressed her lips shut.

"Don't be embarrassed. It's normal for our kind, and it's nothing I haven't felt before."

"I felt horny as hell."

Now it was my turn to blush. I remembered that vividly, too. "You were in heat. That's a wolf thing, too, but that's not the feeling we're looking for. Do you remember anything else about how you felt?"

"I felt hungry, and irritable. I thought it was just that time of the month, but it was more intense than normal. I felt edgy, like I wanted to run or fight. I felt fierce and powerful."

I grinned, remembering my own first shift. I felt the exact same way, but I knew what it meant, and I welcomed it. "That's it. That was your wolf, wanting out. She's still inside you, she's just sedated. You need to wake her up. Try to call forth that part of you."

Luna closed her eyes again and stood still and quiet for several moments before growling in frustration. "I can't feel it anymore."

"It's the middle of the day, and we're past the full moon phase. It's challenging for a mature wolf. But you're just a pup, and your human body has been dominant your whole life. You might not be able to shift till the next full moon."

"I'm not giving up that easily. I'm the boss, not the stupid wolf. It needs to learn to listen to me."

"Don't think of it as a separate being. It's not. It's part of you. You don't command it to obey you so much as you embrace that part of you and let it out instead of repressing it." She looked at me like I was a self-help guru spouting vague, useless, inspirational platitudes then huffed and shut her eyes again.

"Okay, I'm channeling my wolf. Be the wolf." She scrunched up her face and squeezed her hands into fists, tightening her whole body.

"Can you feel her inside you—her power, her energy? Do you feel that fierceness you felt before?"

She concentrated so hard, she was practically vibrating, and her head looked like it would explode, but nothing happened. After several minutes, she released the tension in her body with a growl. "I feel like punching someone again, but I think that's just frustration. Why can't I do this? My wolf was more than ready to come out a few days ago. In fact, I couldn't shift back without help from my dad. Why can't I bring it out now, when I need it?"

"Don't be upset with yourself, Luna. You're tired, stressed, probably hungry."

She nodded and rubbed her belly. It growled in agreement. She let her duffel fall to the ground with a thud then dug in it and pulled out a squished granola bar that looked like it had been laying in the bottom of the bag for months. "This is all I've got, but I'm not sure I even want it. I don't know why I didn't think to bring food."

"I can shift and catch us something if you don't mind eating it raw."

Her face perked up at that. "Sounds better than this." She tossed the granola bar aside.

I started to strip off my clothes, and she dropped her head, but I could tell she was peeking up through her lashes. I couldn't help but smile. "You can watch if you want. You seemed to enjoy it before."

She huffed and turned her head away. "That wasn't me. I was under the influence of powerful werewolf hormones."

Once I was naked, I stepped in front of her so she had nowhere to look but at me. "So, you don't like how I look when you're not a wolf?"

She slowly raised her head, letting her eyes trail up my body. I wasn't shy. I knew I looked good. Most girls thought I was hot. Luna could've gone for one of the other wolves if she wasn't into me. It would've been a lot smarter on her part. The fact that she didn't told me she definitely found me appealing. I wasn't above using my looks to win her over.

She blushed as her gaze lingered on my most impressive parts then slowly lifted to my eyes. "I wouldn't mind watching you shift again. Maybe it will help me learn how to do it."

I could work with that. I made a show of flexing as I slowly felt my wolf rise up inside me. When I couldn't contain it any longer, I let it out with a powerful burst of energy, my human flesh and bones exploding and recombining into wolf parts, the sum ending up much greater than the parts. Luna gasped and scuttled backwards.

I stood in front of her for a moment, letting her get her fill. Her eyes explored every inch of my wolf without any reservation. I'd never given much thought to how my wolf looked, but I could tell she appreciated it.

When my nose caught the musky scent of a deer, I darted off into the woods after it. I had enough practice hunting that it was easy to catch a small fawn in one leap. It didn't even see me coming. I carried it back to Luna between my teeth then dropped my kill at her feet. She gulped and cringed at the sight of it.

It was easier to skin in wolf form, so I moved between Luna and the deer so she wouldn't have to watch as I peeled off a strip of fur with my teeth then tore out a chunk of meat. I turned back to her, gently cradling the meat between my fangs, then stuck out my snout to present it to her. When she held out a hand, I dropped the steaming hunk into her palm. Blood oozed from it, dripping through her fingers and filling the air with its hot, metallic scent.

She looked at it warily for a moment then sniffed it and took a tiny taste. Her wrinkled face relaxed. "Oh wow. It's so warm, it's like a rare steak. It's delicious."

She swallowed the bite then quickly took another. I bit off a hunk for myself, happy and proud that I could satisfy her. We ate in silence for several minutes, our eager groans and chewing the only sound.

When we had our fill, Luna pulled a water bottle from her bag and took a few gulps before offering it to me. I opened my mouth, and she poured the rest of it in. I didn't think she'd had enough, but she didn't seem to have any more.

In my wolf form, I could hear the faint sounds of running water, though. I took the bottle from her, careful not to puncture it, then dashed off to find the stream and refill it. She smiled when I came back with it mostly full, having only spilled a little on the way back. She drank the rest of it, correctly assuming I'd satisfied my own thirst at the stream.

When the bottle was empty, she let out a contented sigh. "I feel a lot better now. Thank you."

I chuffed in response. I was about to shift back to human so I could talk to her again when Luna sat up and stared at me. Then she got to her feet and ran her hand along my flank and over my back. My fur quivered under her touch.

"Do you think you could climb the mountain with me on your back?"

I wasn't sure, but I would break my back trying. She was thin; I could bench press her weight as a human, and I was a lot stronger as a wolf. I lowered myself to my belly so she could climb on.

"I don't think I can balance both duffels and hold onto you at the same time."

I shook my head and picked up my duffel with my

mouth. She slung her duffel strap across her torso and tossed it behind her then threw her leg over my back and grabbed onto my fur. Then we were off.

I savored the warmth and weight of her on me and the way she clung around my neck. It made me feel powerful and needed, and like I was in charge for once. And in my wolf form, it took no effort to climb the mountain with her on my back. I leapt up the craggy rocks and threaded through the dense forest with ease, my strong legs eating up the distance. We should've thought of this a long time ago. What would've taken hours in human form took only minutes as a wolf.

Luna whooped and hollered in excitement, and I bellowed out a howl that echoed through the trees, frightening off other creatures. A huge bird squawked loudly at us as it passed overhead, its shadow blocking out the sun for a moment. I was so caught up in the thrill of the run, I didn't realize we had reached the summit till I stumbled over it.

CHAPTER 15

NIKKO

My claws dug into the rock, scrambling for purchase, as I fought to keep myself from falling over the edge, but Luna didn't have a tight enough grip to stop herself from flying forward. She sailed over my head, her body somersaulting. I watched in horror as she tumbled down the backside of the peak, thudding gruesomely as she bounced off large boulders and pinballed between trees.

After several long, agonizing seconds, she rolled to a stop. Her body lay limp and lifeless at the bottom of the mountain. I stared at it for a moment, dumbstruck, before leaping down the cliff after her, mindless of my own safety. I pounded onto the ground beside her, shaking it and her, but she didn't move. A loud, tortured howl escaped me. Was she dead because of my carelessness?

Her arm lay draped over her hip. I nudged it with my snout, but all it did was flop beside her at an awkward angle. She didn't cry out, even though the bone was obviously broken. One of her legs was twisted, too. What else was broken?

I stuck my nose up to hers and held my breath, trying to determine if she was breathing. A gasp ripped from my throat when I felt a tiny stream of warm air. She was still alive!

In her human form, she needed immediate medical attention. But we were miles from any kind of civilization. If she could shift, her body would heal itself in the process, but there was no way she could shift now. Even if she knew how, she couldn't do anything while she was unconscious.

I was going to have to get her to a hospital, but how? The only way I could carry her as a wolf was with my teeth. I carefully scooped her up in my mouth, but her body flopped around like a rag doll. If I ran, all the jostling might injure her worse. I carefully set her back down. Could I make a stretcher or sling out of something? Maybe I should run back to town and get the hospital to send a helicopter for her.

I was so distracted, trying to think of a solution, I didn't even notice the giant bird circling overhead till it swooped down and landed beside me with a squawk so loud it echoed off the mountains and reverberated throughout the entire valley. My head jerked up and kept tilting back to scan the full height of him, but my body froze in shock.

With a white head, a yellow beak large enough to crack my skull open, claws like meat hooks, and a wingspan of at least ten feet, he looked like an eagle but was twice as big. But it was his back end that proved he was no regular bird. His dark wings gave way to tawny brown fur that covered the hind legs and tail of a lion. I'd seen pictures of creatures like him before, but only in mythology books. Werewolves were legends, too, though, so why couldn't gryphons be just as real as werewolves were?

He glared at me with intense yellow eyes then opened his beak and let out a menacing squawk. He flapped his massive wings as he moved towards me, stirring up enough wind to ruffle my fur. Was he trying to scare me off? Did he think Luna was a tasty morsel he could steal?

I leapt between them and barked threateningly at him, but that only made him angrier. How on earth was I going to get rid of this guy so I could help Luna? I barked and growled some more, moving closer to him. I didn't want to attack him because I wasn't positive I would win. It would only take one snap of that beak to bite my head off.

He flapped his wings some more, but this time he scuttled backwards. I lunged towards him again, and he spread his wings and took off. I let out a loud howl, feeling victorious. But before I had a chance to turn back to Luna, he flew in a circle, swooped down behind me, and grabbed her with his giant claws, lifting her off the ground. In seconds, they were a hundred feet in the air and flying quickly.

I felt like my heart was being dragged along with them. It beat frantically, trying to keep up, and I took off after them, baying in anger. My legs stretched to their limit as I bounded over long stretches of land. I was going so fast, my paws barely touched the ground. With my body airborne for several seconds with each leap, it was as close to flying as I could get. I kept my head up, barely watching where I was running as my eyes followed the gryphon through the sky. It was a miracle I didn't crash into anything.

I skidded to a stop when I broke through the trees and an honest-to-God stone castle came into view. The gryphon flew in a circle over it then disappeared behind a turret. I raced around the backside of the castle, but they were gone. Had he flown inside the castle? Was that where he roosted?

I ran back around to the front, leapt up the stone steps, and threw myself at the wide, double doors, clawing at the wood and barking my head off like a rabid animal. It felt cathartic, but it wasn't very effective, so after a few moments I looked around for a window or another door that I could get in. As if on cue, a window opened above me, and a gorgeous, pale, teenage girl with white blonde hair stuck her head out and gawked at me.

As defenseless as I felt as a human, I figured I might have better luck getting inside if I could explain myself, so on impulse, I shifted. The girl shrieked, but instead of acting scared, she clapped her hands and smiled excitedly, looking me up and down. I quickly covered my privates.

"Oh my God, are you a werewolf? Mara, come look!"

"A gryphon just carried my mate into this castle," I bellowed. I sounded like a madman.

The girl frowned and turned her head to talk to someone behind her. I growled when she moved away from the window, and I was about to jump up there when a second girl, this one with dark brown hair, olive skin, and a dark mole above full, black cherry lips, poked her head around the window frame. She stared suspiciously at me.

"Please, let me in so I can find my mate. He just took

her from me," I begged. Anxiety rippled through my body, making me jittery. I probably looked like a crazed drug addict.

The blonde girl squeezed in next to the dark-haired girl to gawk at me some more. Standing together, the two girls looked like an angel and a devil, one dressed like a goth princess in black layers and the other in a white sweater and pink jeans.

"I'm gonna go down and check him out. He's cute," the blonde said.

Mara grabbed her arm to stop her and glared at me. "I don't trust him. Aras wouldn't take the girl unless he thought she was in danger."

"She fell, and she's badly hurt. She needs medical attention."

"I'm going to go find Aras. Watch this guy. Don't let him try anything." The dark-haired girl disappeared.

The blonde cradled her chin in her hands and leaned her elbows on the windowsill. She looked so innocent and angelic, I didn't know how she could stop me if I did try anything. "What's your name, wolf boy?"

I sighed. I had no desire to chat, but there wasn't much else I could do at the moment unless I wanted to jump through the window. "Nikko. What's yours?"

"I'm Lorelei. I'm a siren." She smiled sweetly at me and sat down on the window ledge.

I tensed and backed up. So that was why the other girl had left her on guard duty. I wouldn't have believed her, but after seeing a gryphon, it didn't seem any more implausible. Apparently, I'd found the supernatural sanctuary that Luna was looking for.

A moment later, the large front doors opened with a

loud creak. I whipped my head around to see a white-haired man dressed in black walking out with a younger, darker-haired version of himself beside him, both with predatory, yellow eyes that narrowed in on me like flash-light beams. I hurried over to them, keeping my hands in front of me. Nudity was no big deal around the pack, but I tried to avoid it around strangers.

"My name is Andor, and this is my son, Aras. He claims you were attacking a human. You are a wolf?" the old man asked me, his deep voice and wizened appearance commanding respect.

"Yes, sir. I mean, no, sir. Argh!" I yanked a hand through my hair in frustration.

"Yes, I'm a wolf. No, I wasn't attacking the girl. She's a wolf, too, and my mate. But she fell, and she's injured. I was trying to figure out how to get her back to town without causing more injury when your son swooped in and took her." I glared at him.

The younger man shrugged guiltily. "He had her in his mouth. It looked like he was going to eat her."

I shook my head and rolled my eyes at him. I didn't feel any of the same need to respect him like I did his father.

Andor ignored my reaction and said, "Wolves can heal themselves, can they not? If the girl is a wolf, why hasn't she healed already?"

"We can only heal when we shift. She's a pup; she doesn't know how to control her wolf yet. Please, let me take her to a hospital. She needs medical attention."

Aras crossed his arms over his chest. "There's no hospital anywhere near here. That's why I brought her here. What were you two doing out here, anyway? This is private land. There aren't any wolf packs in these parts."

"We were actually looking for this place, I think. We needed somewhere safe to hide out. Luna's father heard about this place and sent us here."

"Your name?"

"Nikko Brisbane, and my mate is Luna Ammon."

Andor nodded and gestured towards the door. "Come, let's go see the girl…"

Aras grabbed his father's arm to stop him. "How do we know he's telling the truth? The girl's unconscious."

"There are enough supernaturals here to defend our home against one wolf, should he have an ulterior motive," Andor replied and kept walking. I hurried after him, up the stone steps and into the castle.

Aras glared at me and followed us. "Two wolves, if what he says is true." Once inside, he slammed the door shut behind us with an ominous thud.

The musty smell of the dank castle didn't completely cover the pungent scent of creatures I couldn't recognize. Who all lived here? The interior walls were the same thick stone as on the outside, making me wonder how they'd run wires to the gold sconces mounted on them. The place looked like it predated electricity by a couple centuries. The dark, hardwood floors shined with a glossy patina but were scarred with at least a hundred years of wear, including some fierce-looking claw marks.

The large entryway opened to an even larger hall with stone staircases curving up either side. The two girls from the window hurried down one set of stairs to meet us. Andor pointed at them. "This is Lorelei and Mara. One of you get Orson, will you? Where's Cassius?"

I wondered what kind of supe Mara was, but no one volunteered that information, nor who Orson or Cassius were or why Andor wanted them. But the way Lorelei and Mara argued over who had to go fetch Orson worried me. My imagination ran wild, making me nervous. I was used to being the most dangerous creature around, but here was a whole castle full of potential rivals.

"What's all the noise? What's going on? I'm trying to sleep up here." A rumbly voice bellowed from upstairs. A huge man with thick, dark hair covering every exposed inch of his skin appeared at the top of the other staircase. Mara sidled up to him and ran a hand down his chest, scratching at his chest hair with long, black-painted nails.

"Hi, Orson. Nice of you to join us," she murmured. His face softened into a goofy smile, and he wrapped his arms around her.

Andor led us up the stairs towards him. "Orson, we have some guests. This is Nikko. He's a werewolf. Aras brought his injured mate here. We're going to check on her. Why don't you come with us?"

Orson let us pass then took up the rear, looming a head taller and twice as broad as the rest of us.

"Do you want me to go find Cassius?" Lorelei asked.

Andor shook his head. "I'm not sure that's a good idea."

At the end of the hall, we climbed another set of stairs leading up into the turret, this one narrow and winding. I felt claustrophobic, surrounded by stone and penned in by supernatural creatures I knew only from storybooks. Windows looked out over the expanse of land surrounding the castle, but they were too small to escape through. I half expected to find Rapunzel dangling her hair from one of them.

Another odor I didn't recognize caught my attention, making the hair on my arms stand up. My heart rate quickened, my body tensed, and my wolf roared to life inside me. It took all my willpower to hold him back. When I heard a hiss, a roar, and the bone-crunching, flesh-tearing sound of a wolf shifting, I lost control, and my own wolf exploded out of me. I leapt up the stairs towards Luna.

CHAPTER 16

LUNA

You know how it feels when you wake up from a nightmare, heart pounding, body shaking, and it takes a minute to convince yourself it wasn't real? Well, this was like the exact opposite of that.

One second there was nothing. Darkness, silence, no sensation. I might as well have been dead. Then the next second, pain ripped through me as my body exploded. Suddenly, I was wide awake, terrified, and panting. I was a wolf again. I tried to convince myself it was only a dream, but it wasn't. There was a predator in the room with me. My body knew it even though my mind still felt fuzzy.

Standing in the corner, mouth hanging open, was a teenage guy with pale skin, black hair, and dark eyes, dressed like a goth hipster in a black, cowl-neck sweater and dark jeans rolled up over black Timberlands. While slightly creepy looking, he didn't look especially danger-ous, but something about him had my hackles raised and my wolf ready to attack. His scent was enough to drive me into a frenzy. I growled and barked at him, and he held his hands up in front of himself and backed into the corner.

Suddenly, another wolf bounded into the room, howling. Nikko. A wave of relief washed over me. He raced over to me, running his snout up and down my flank, sniffing. Then he whipped around to search out the threat, guarding me with his body. He snarled and growled and barked at the guy in the corner. Saliva dripped from his bared fangs as he snapped his jaws.

But before either one of them could attack the other, a giant grizzly bear charged in. He roared and rose up on his hind legs, at least ten feet tall and flashing enormous claws and fangs. Nikko, the guy in the corner, and I all froze. The only sound was our heavy breathing.

A moment later, an old man burst into the room. Another teenage guy came in behind him, followed by two girls. They whipped their heads back and forth between me, Nikko, the bear, and the creepy guy, assessing the situation. The old man held out his hands and slowly stepped forward. "Cassius, leave the room, please."

The creepy guy sidled carefully towards the door, not taking his eyes off us. He squeezed past everyone in the doorway and disappeared down the stairs. Once he was gone, the bear dropped down onto all fours, still staring at us, but less threateningly. Was this the sanctuary? If so, it didn't feel very safe. And why didn't I remember how I got there?

The old man turned his attention to Nikko and me. "Cassius is a vampire. I'm well aware of the enmity between your kind. I will not allow him or anyone else to harm you, but I expect the same from you. Please return to your human form so we can communicate."

I stiffened and looked to Nikko. Nikko glanced warily back and forth between me, the old man, and the stairs while everyone watched us. Eventually, he shifted back into human form. It was just as fascinating to watch. The two girls by the stairs seemed a little too curious about Nikko's body, though. I glared at them, and a growl rumbled in the back of my throat.

As soon as Nikko was human again, all eyes turned towards me. I whined and ducked my head behind him. He stroked my chest over my still-pounding heart, and I nudged my head against him.

"She doesn't know how to shift back yet. It might take a while before she's calm enough to let go of her wolf."

"That's alright. I can see she trusts you. I apologize for my son's hasty reaction." The old man flicked his eyes towards the younger guy who hung his head.

"We'll give you two a little time alone."

Everyone else reluctantly turned to leave the room. The old man glanced at the bear and said, "Orson, why don't you wait at the base of the stairs for now and bring our new guests to me when they're ready."

The bear slunk off, thumping down the stairs, his claws scratching on the steps. The old man followed after him, leaving Nikko and me alone in the small, tower-like room. I slumped down onto my belly, exhausted and overwhelmed.

Nikko sat down on the bed beside me and ran a hand down my flank. "I'm so sorry, Luna. Are you okay? Are you in any pain? It was my job to protect you, and I failed. Can you ever forgive me?"

I cocked my head in question.

His face twisted in painful memories. "Don't you remember what happened? You flew off me and fell down the mountain. I thought you were dead at first. You were unconscious, and you had several broken bones. I was trying to figure out how to get help when a gryphon came and snatched you away from me and brought you here."

I tensed at the dramatic explanation. I didn't remember any of that, but maybe that was a good thing. The last thing I remembered was the thrill of riding Nikko's back as he loped up the mountain, my hands gripping his soft fur, the warm sun on my skin, the wind whipping my hair.

"I worried you were too hurt to shift and heal yourself, but I guess the threat of a vampire was enough to force your shift. I'm so glad you're okay." He buried his head in my fur, dampening it with his tears.

Thankfully, my body had healed when I shifted, and there were no lingering effects of my injury. I never would've known I was hurt so badly if Nikko hadn't told me. I had so many questions, though. I wished Nikko would shift back to a wolf so I could communicate with him. But I guess I was the one who needed to shift.

Nikko said I needed to relax before I could shift, so I tried to calm my racing heart and slow my breathing. I was safe, for the moment anyway, and we'd found our way to the sanctuary, even if the journey was a little eventful. Nikko petted me gently, snuggling up against my side. Surprisingly, I felt calm and safe next to him. Despite my resistance towards him, I'd felt that way the whole journey. Eventually, I felt the stress dissipate.

Nikko must've sensed it, too. "Ready to try shifting

back? Just do like you did when you were trying to bring out your wolf. Concentrate on the feeling of being human."

I chuffed then focused my mind on human things. It was a lot easier to imagine. But no matter what I did, none of it had any effect on my body. I whined in frustration and started pacing. I wished my dad was around to command me to shift back like before. It made me wonder if Nikko had an authority over me since he'd claimed me. I suppose if he did, he would've used it.

Instead, he said, "Try to remember a powerful human moment and harness the energy you felt."

My mind immediately went to the memory of leaving my family. All the sadness and hopelessness came flooding back. But all that did was make me want to forget. I needed to think about a positive memory instead. A moment popped into my brain, bringing with it a rush of pleasure, but I immediately squashed it down. Having sex with Nikko was not something I wanted to think about either.

But once the memory was in my head, my brain wouldn't let go of it. The experience played out again, and my body responded like it remembered just as well as my brain did. My heart sped up again, pounding out the rhythm of my desire, and my flesh tingled with electrical currents, desperate for someone to touch me and complete the circuit. I mindlessly rubbed up against Nikko. He stroked my fur and looked at me curiously.

I remembered the feel of his hot hands on my wind-chilled human skin, stroking, kneading. The taste of his lips, devouring mine. His firm muscles pressing against me. That moment of ecstasy when I came undone.

I cried out as the memory overwhelmed me, and suddenly my body exploded again, my flesh and bones remaking themselves. I crumpled to the ground, a lifeless sack of body parts.

Nikko hurried over to me and cradled my head in his arms. "You did it! Great job. Are you okay?"

All I could do was breathe heavily for a few moments. I stared up into his warm, honey eyes as Nikko held me. Something in my gaze must've clued him in to how I was feeling, because he slowly lowered his lips to mine. We kissed gently for several seconds before he pulled away. "Sorry, I shouldn't have taken advantage."

I wanted to tell him it was okay, admit that I liked it, wanted it even. But wanting to kiss him and wanting to be his mate were two very different things, and it wasn't fair of me to lead him on when I wasn't ready to give him what he wanted.

I sat up, pulling my knees up to my chest and wrapping my arms tightly around them. Nikko pulled the blanket off the bed and tossed it over my shoulders. He was naked, too, but he didn't seem to mind. I couldn't resist peeking at him.

A knock sounded on the door, and a young, male voice called out, "I found your duffel bags out in the woods. I'm going to toss them in."

The door opened a crack, and our bags pushed through. Nikko got up and grabbed them. "Thanks."

He handed my bag to me then turned around to give me some privacy. I opened the bag, pulled out the first things I saw, then quickly threw them on. When I turned around, Nikko had dressed, too.

He quirked his lip in a smile. "Ready to go downstairs and meet the other mutants?"

After that wild, first introduction, I wasn't sure this was a safe place for us, after all. But the old man's promise that no one would hurt us repeated in my mind. I looked around at the curved stone walls and glanced out the large window that overlooked the mountains. Where was I?

I sucked in a deep breath. "I guess so."

Nikko headed towards the door, so I followed him down winding stone steps. A large, hairy man sat at the bottom of them. He jumped up and looked at us with dark brown eyes I'd seen before then held out a hand the size of my wolf paw.

"I'm Orson."

I tentatively reached out my own hand, and his engulfed it. "Luna. Are you…?"

"Bear shifter," he answered the question I didn't know how to ask.

Nikko shook his hand and introduced himself, too. Then Orson nodded down the hallway. "Come on, I'll take you to Andor."

We followed him to a large room filled with floor-to-ceiling mahogany bookshelves and several comfortable armchairs. Gold knickknacks dotted every flat surface. The dusty scent of old books made the space feel historic. The old man sat behind a large, antique desk.

He rose as we entered and smiled kindly, extending a hand so bony and leathery it felt more like a claw. "You must be Luna. Glad to see you're alright. I'm Andor. I am a gryphon, and this is my home."

Nikko had mentioned a gryphon earlier, but my brain had skipped over that detail. Now I gawked at him, trying to picture the old man morphing into the mythical creature. My mouth must've been hanging open, because Andor chuckled at me.

"I'm sorry, I'm just new to all this. I didn't even know werewolves existed until a few days ago. Now vampires, bear shifters, and gryphons? I thought that was all fairytale stuff."

"Don't apologize. I'm glad the human world has relegated my kind to legend. Gryphons were hunted almost to extinction a long time ago, and we sought refuge in remote places like this. My son and I settled here a few hundred years ago after I lost his mother. Eventually, we opened our home to other supernatural creatures in need of sanctuary. Tell me, why did you come here?"

I knew he needed to know our story so he could decide whether or not to let us stay, but I really didn't feel like airing our dirty laundry for a stranger. Besides, if I told him the whole truth, he might not trust Nikko, and I realized I wanted him there with me. Better the devil you know than the devil you don't. I was frantically trying to think up a convincing half truth when Nikko spoke up.

"Luna is the first she-wolf in generations, so a lot of wolves want her. Our packs are fighting over her."

Andor murmured sympathetically, and I let out my breath. "Well, I'm happy to provide sanctuary for you, as long as you agree to live peacefully with the others."

"Who all lives here?" Nikko asked the same question on the tip of my tongue.

Andor took a seat in one of the armchairs and gestured for us to do the same. "There are seven of us presently. Besides myself and my son, Orson has been here the longest. I found him as a cub. His mother had been shot by a human."

I glanced sympathetically towards the giant man who looked more like a cuddly teddy bear in his human form even though he was enormous.

"Several years later, my son saw Lorelei on an outcropping of rocks by the ocean, luring the sailors. Sirens are quite appealing, even to those who aren't affected by their song. He fancied her and convinced her to come and stay with us."

I gulped, and my eyes got big. Andor smiled reassuringly at me. "Don't worry. Her powers don't seem to have any effect on other supernaturals."

"Mara's the one you need to worry about," Orson grumbled from the corner. I flicked my eyes to Andor for confirmation.

He shook his head. "Mara is a witch, but her inability to control her powers forced her into hiding. She knows better than to practice spells on any of the other residents."

His vagueness left me curious what had happened. Did she blow up her school or turn somebody into a frog? It sounded like the plot line of a CW show.

That left the vampire and one other. What other mythical creature was alive and well and living in this castle? Possibilities ping-ponged through my mind.

"Like most teenagers, Cassius, too, struggled to control his urges. He was unable to assimilate in human society and settle down in any one place. During his travels, he found us. None of us are a temptation to him like humans are."

Nikko said vampires were our natural prey, but the

way my wolf reacted to him, he felt more like a predator. They must have some kind of defense against us if Cassius wasn't afraid to snoop around my bed while I was unconscious. My ignorance left me feeling vulnerable. I needed to quiz Nikko on vampires as soon as I had a chance.

While my thoughts wandered, Andor continued, "Lastly, we have Jinx, a fairy changeling whose parents rejected him when they suspected his true nature. He was happy to have a new family."

Andor glanced at a tall grandfather clock in the corner when it chimed 6 pm. "It's nearing dinner time. Why don't you join us, and you can get to know everyone?"

Nikko and I exchanged a nervous glance then nodded. I still wasn't sure about this castle full of fairytale creatures, but it seemed as good a place as any for two werewolves on the run. Nikko held out a hand, and I took it, glad I wasn't doing this alone.

Andor smiled. "Let's go to the dining room."

He led us down the hall to a wide, stone staircase with wrought iron railings that curved along the walls of a large hall with ceilings so high they were in shadow. At the bottom of the stairs, he turned down another hallway but stopped outside a room with a dark wood table big enough to seat a dozen people and filled with enough food for twice that many. High back chairs upholstered in aged, red velvet lined both sides. Andor's son and the two girls were already there, as well as Cassius.

My body tensed, and I hissed and grabbed onto Nikko. My wolf quivered, threatening to explode out of me. From the tightness in Nikko's muscles, I assumed he was feeling the same way.

Andor must've sensed our tension. "Cassius is a resident here. If you wish to stay, you'll have to learn to control your impulses around him, and I'll expect him to do the same. It might be difficult at first, but I have confidence that even wolves and vampires can live in harmony if they choose. I won't allow anyone to stay here if I believe they are a threat."

Cassius got up and headed towards us, making the hair on my arms stand up. I gritted my teeth and forced myself to stay still even though my body was vibrating with nervous energy. He didn't extend his hand, but he did offer a shaky smile. He looked as human as anyone else, and if my wolf wasn't chomping at the bit to attack him, I never would've guessed he was a vampire.

"I'm Cassius. I'm sorry I scared you earlier. I was just too curious to resist spying on you. I've never met a werewolf before."

Now that I knew what he was, I was curious, too. But I didn't have enough control of my wolf yet to have a chat with him. He must've sensed my fragile control, because he hurried away and took a seat on the far side of the table.

I glanced around at the other residents, who were staring at us curiously. All of them had dangerous, supernatural powers I didn't fully understand. I didn't know if I could trust any of them. The only person I felt safe with was Nikko, and a few hours ago, he was my biggest enemy. Could I be safe here, or was I making another huge mistake?

CHAPTER 17

LUNA

"Sit next to me, Luna." The blonde siren patted the chair beside her, a wide smile lighting her angelic face. Her smile seemed almost too friendly, aggressive even. I couldn't think of a reason to say no that wouldn't risk offending her, though, so I slid into the chair. I gave a hesitant smile back to her and to the other girl sitting across from her, who stared me down like her silvery eyes could see into my soul. Her gaze shifted to Nikko as he sat down beside me, and her eyes softened a little.

"I'm Lorelei, and that's Mara. This is Aras." Lorelei wrapped a hand around the arm of the young guy beside her, the one I assumed was Andor's son. I wasn't sure if he owed me an apology or I owed him a thank you, so I just nodded at him.

Suddenly, a small boy with spiky, blond hair wearing a purple smock over green and blue striped tights appeared beside me, like magic. I jumped and yelped. Thankfully, my wolf didn't feel threatened enough to make an appearance, but my blood pulsed in my ears.

Lorelei leaned past me and scowled at him. "Jinx, you shouldn't scare people like that! It's not nice."

"This coming from the girl who lures men to their death?" Jinx said, his voice dripping with sarcasm, and rolled his bright green eyes. Now that I had a better look at him, I realized he wasn't a child, after all, but more like a miniature man.

Lorelei huffed. "I can't help it; it's a biological imperative! But I don't do it anymore. I'm reformed. Unlike some people, I try to control my impulses."

The tension between them made me nervous, especially since I was in its path. I tried to diffuse it by changing the subject, but I only opened Pandora's box. "Jinx? Is that your real name?"

The tiny man-boy narrowed his eyes at me and disappeared then reappeared on the other side of the room, hovering midair. "Of course not. Do you think I'm an idiot?"

Andor frowned at him. "Manners please, Jinx."

I glanced around, confused. Cassius filled me in. "He's a fairy. They believe knowing their real name gives a person power over them."

It sounded absurd, but no more so than any of the other crazy stuff I'd seen in the last few days. The last thing I needed was another enemy, so I smiled gently at him and said, "I'm sorry, Jinx. I didn't mean to upset you. I don't know anything about fairies. I don't even know much about werewolves."

"Did you wolf out by accident and hurt someone? Is that why you're on the run?" Mara the witch asked. Her tone made it sound like she hoped it was true. The others perked up, excited to hear the story.

I opened my mouth to give the carefully edited explanation that Nikko had offered to Andor, but it got stuck in my throat. It seemed conceited to claim that I was so special that packs were fighting over me. Fortunately, Nikko stepped in again and answered for me. "Our packs are fighting, and it wasn't safe for us there."

Lorelei widened her pale, aqua eyes and put a hand on her forehead like she was going to swoon. "You're from enemy packs? Is it like a Romeo and Juliet thing between you two?"

It reminded me of what my friend Macy has said about Nikko and me. I felt a painful pinch in my chest that I might never get to see her again. I hadn't even had a chance to say goodbye.

Andor spoke up before I could formulate a response. "I doubt our guests wish to discuss their love life with strangers. Let's respect their privacy. Shall we eat?"

Mara and Lorelei frowned at him like he was ruining all the fun, but they didn't argue with him. Instead, they glanced suspiciously at Jinx and filled their plates.

The foods I used to love didn't appeal to me as much now that I was a wolf, but I was eager to change the subject, so I said, "Dinner looks amazing. Who's the chef?"

"Everyone takes turns making the meals. Tonight was Jinx's turn." Mara gave him a menacing glare I didn't understand until I took a bite of the chicken.

It tasted like rotten eggs and turned to gooey chalk in my mouth like it was made of plaster. My eyes watered, and my first instinct was to spit it out. But I forced myself to swallow it down and gritted my teeth to keep from gagging. I didn't know it was possible to ruin meat that badly. How on earth was I going to stomach it?

I didn't have to worry for long, though, because within seconds the rest of the table had the same, intense reaction, only they didn't hide it. They gagged and coughed and spit it out onto napkins, their hands, even their plates. All except for Jinx, who started laughing hysterically, a high, trilling sound like bells ringing.

"It's not funny, Jinx! You know you're not supposed to use your magic on us!" Mara complained.

Orson jumped up and roared at him, the teddy bear turning into a grizzly, in spirit if not physically. Although, the way he was shaking, it looked like he might shift any minute. "You ruined our dinner on purpose? I'm hungry! What are we supposed to eat now?"

Jinx didn't even flinch at the huge man looming over him. "You're always hungry, Orson! You eat like you're getting ready to hibernate. It wouldn't kill you to skip a meal."

"Enough!" Andor pounded the table, and everyone quieted.

"Jinx, I've warned you before about this. Please leave the table. I'll speak to you later."

Jinx rolled his eyes. "Oh come on! It was hilarious! And harmless."

The way Andor glared at him, his yellow eyes flashing, I thought he might shift and carry him off in his talons. Jinx grumbled under his breath then disappeared.

Andor sighed and shook his head as he looked at Nikko and me. "I'm sorry you had to experience that. I do not allow any of the residents here to use their powers against one another. I will not stand for that, not even in jest. There will be consequences for his behavior."

I didn't want to ask what he meant by that. But the

way everyone else got quiet made it clear he was serious. It was reassuring and intimidating at the same time. I didn't know how to control my abilities yet. What if I did something wrong?

He turned to Mara and said, "We are in need of a speedy dinner. I'm sure our guests are hungry. Do you think you can whip something up?"

I thought she might go into the kitchen, but instead, she stood up and pulled a wand out of a sheath hanging from a leather belt around her waist. Sucking in a deep breath, she waved the wand over the table and said, "Cibus evanescet."

Suddenly, all the food disappeared. I gasped and laid a hand on my empty plate, but it didn't feel empty. It felt lumpy and squishy. I jerked my hand away and wiped the invisible gunk on my napkin.

Andor saw what I did, poked at his own plate, then pinched something and picked it up, prodding it with a finger. "Close, but not quite, Mara. Why don't you try again?"

The others started laughing at her and jabbing at the invisible food on their own plates. Mara frowned then carefully touched her plate. Her cheeks turned red, and she quickly waved her wand again. "Cibus abire!"

I waited for someone else to touch their plate that time before checking to see if my plate was as empty as it looked. Once Andor was sure the spell had worked properly, he said, "Why don't you try conjuring up a nice salmon for me, Mara."

She tried a few spells before she landed on the right one, first creating a realistic-looking fish that was nothing but an image, then conjuring up a live one that immediately flopped off the plate and onto the floor. Lorelei happily snatched it up and ate it.

Eventually, Andor had a tasty, baked salmon on his plate. Orson and Aras wanted the same thing, so she conjured some for them, too. Then she turned to Nikko and cooed, "What can I get for you?"

"I'd love a rare steak if you can do it. But if not, a salmon would be fine."

"Same here," I piped up.

She waved her wand, mumbled something, then squeaked out a cheer, as excited as we were when she got it right on the first try and a juicy, pink steak appeared on Nikko's plate. She conjured up one more for me then turned to Cassius.

Cassius wiggled his eyebrows. "Umm, can I get a still-beating human heart? If that's too much trouble, I'll just take the whole human."

Andor scowled at him then looked at Mara. "He'll have a rare steak, as well."

"You spoil all the fun," Cassius grumbled.

She conjured up a steak for Cassius, then we all took tentative tastes of our food. I happily chewed and swallowed when I discovered it actually tasted good. "Thank you, Mara. This is great."

"Yeah, this is amazing," Nikko said.

Her lips curled in a wide smile, and she leaned forward and peeked up at him through her lashes. "You really like it?"

He nodded, and mumbled around a huge mouthful of steak, "Absolutely. I can't believe you can wave a wand and conjure up food like this. It's incredible."

"I'll make you whatever you want whenever you

want it, Nikko. Just ask," she murmured, pushing out her chest. She didn't extend the same offer to anyone else.

I focused on chewing so I wouldn't growl at her. I didn't know why I felt jealous that she was flirting with him. A few days ago, I wanted to get as far away from Nikko as possible. And although I didn't despise him as much as I did then, I still wasn't in love with him, or anything. Regardless, I wasn't going to risk upsetting her or giving Nikko any ideas by staking my claim over him.

The others bantered back and forth as they ate, joking about the unusual dinner, but I stayed quiet, just grateful I wasn't the topic of conversation. I finished my steak quickly and wished I had more, but I didn't feel comfortable asking Mara to conjure up a second one for me. Nikko noticed my empty plate and the look of longing on my face, though.

"Luna, are you still hungry? Do you want some more? I'm sure Mara would be happy to make you another one."

The look on Mara's face told me she wasn't happy about the way Nikko was fawning over me. What was her deal?

"If it's no trouble," I said, plastering on a saccharine smile.

Andor must've caught the tension between us because he gave Mara a stern look. "We're a family here. We help each other in whatever way we can. That extends to both of you, if you'd like to stay here."

Nikko and I exchanged a silent look. This place might be full of strange creatures, but it was our best option at the moment. I turned to Andor and said, "Thank you. We would."

Andor gave a welcoming smile. "We'll find a room for you right after dinner."

He turned to Mara and said, "Give our new friends a second helping. They've had a long day."

Mara forced back a snarl and conjured up more steak for us. I took a small, first bite, just in case she decided to vent her irritation through the food, but it tasted fine. Maybe I was imagining her attitude.

After dinner, Andor led us upstairs and down a hallway lined with bedrooms. He stopped at one halfway down then opened the door and ushered us in. My eyes scanned the large space, taking in the fringed, oriental rug, the antique cherry furniture, and the tapestry decorating one of the stone walls. But it was the bed beneath it that captured my attention. One bed in the center of the room.

"This is the only empty room with a bed big enough for two. Will this suit?"

I opened my mouth to protest, but Nikko shot me a warning look and spoke up before I got out any words. "This is great, Andor. Thanks so much."

Nikko must've told him that we were mated. I shut my mouth, not wanting to contradict whatever story he told Andor and risk his trust, but I gave Nikko a look that promised he'd be hearing about this later.

"There are bathrooms down the hall to your left. I'll have Aras bring your things from the tower. If you need anything, don't hesitate to ask. I'll let you get some rest now. I'm sure you're exhausted. Breakfast will be available whenever you wake up."

As soon as Andor left, I shut the door and whipped

around towards Nikko, dropping my smile. "Why did you tell him we were mated?"

"Aras thought I was attacking you. That's why he snatched you from me. I had to convince them to trust me."

I threw my hands in the air. "But now they expect us to act like mates!"

He stepped closer and gave me a cocky smile. "Is that so bad?"

I pushed past him and flopped on the bed with my arms and legs spread wide, taking up the whole space. "You might think so after a few nights of sleeping on the floor."

He huffed then sighed. "Fine. But you can't tell them…"

I sat up and glared at him. "Tell them what? The truth? That you claimed me against my will before I even knew what you were doing? Yeah, they might not trust you so much if I told them that. I know the feeling."

He sat down beside me on a tiny, open corner of the bed. "I already told you how sorry I am about what I did. Will you ever forgive me? I can't change it, Luna. All I can do is try to make it up to you by protecting you."

I wanted to insist that I didn't need or want his protection, but the truth was, I was scared and lonely and overwhelmed by all of this. Having someone there with me, even someone like Nikko, was better than dealing with this on my own. I didn't like showing weakness, though, so I wasn't about to admit any of that.

I twisted my scowl into a quirky grin then grabbed a pillow and smacked him with it. "You're still sleeping on the floor, though. Lay by the door so that vampire can't get in."

Aras delivered our duffel bags a few minutes later, then Nikko and I went searching for the bathrooms to get ready for bed. Small, wooden plaques hung from the doors, differentiating the ladies' room from the men's.

I flinched when I walked inside and saw Mara standing at the wide, gold-veined marble vanity, using one of the two sinks. I flicked her a small smile then hurried past and used one of the stalls, hoping she'd leave before I was done. But she was still standing there when I came out, slathering her face with moisturizer from a tiny jar that looked like it cost a fortune but she'd probably conjured up with a wave of her wand. Even without her makeup on, she was still beautiful.

I washed my hands and stared at our reflections in the mirror. I looked frumpy in comparison, with my fair skin deathly pale from all the stress, dark circles under my eyes, and my hair a tangled mess. Mara gave me a once-over, and her grimace told me she thought the same thing.

"I've never met a werewolf before. Does it hurt when you shift? It looks like it's exhausting."

I didn't have any fancy potions to improve my skin, so I pulled out a hairbrush and tried to tame my snarled mane instead. "It hurts, but it feels good at the same time. Like I'm breaking out of a confined space. It feels powerful and freeing to let the animal out of its cage."

She didn't flinch in fear or cower in intimidation like I hoped she would. Instead, she smirked and said, "I'd like to watch. Will you shift for me? If it's no trouble."

Before I could respond, she widened her eyes exaggeratedly and put a hand to her mouth. "Oh wait, I forgot. You don't know how yet. Nikko said you're just a puppy."

I narrowed my eyes at her in the mirror and bit back a growl. She gave a cocky smile back. "Maybe Nikko will shift for me. Do you know which room he's in?"

I stuck the hairbrush back in my bag and yanked the door open, ignoring the fact that I hadn't brushed my teeth or changed into my pajamas. "Yeah, two doors down on the right. Same one as me, since he's my mate."

CHAPTER 18

NIKKO

Luna yanked the door open, stomped inside, then slammed it shut behind her. Was there steam curling from her ears, or was that just my imagination? She still had her jeans on, even though she'd gone to the bathroom to change into her pajamas.

"Did something happen?" I dared to ask her but stayed on the other side of the room because she looked like she wanted to rip someone's head off, presumably mine since I'd been public enemy number one ever since that fateful night in the woods.

"That Mara is an obnoxious skank. She's attracted to you, and she's being blatantly obvious about it, even though she knows you're my mate! She thinks she can take whatever she wants."

As angry as Luna was, I couldn't help the smile that crept up my cheeks. Maybe she hadn't admitted to herself that she wanted me yet, but she clearly didn't want anyone else to have me. Her possessive attitude gave me hope that maybe she was warming up to me more than she let on.

"I'll make sure she knows I'm already taken."

She crossed her arms over her chest and stamped her foot repeatedly. "I just don't like her attitude. She acts like she'd like to take me out to get to you!"

"I won't let her touch you." I slowly moved closer and put a hand on her arm to calm her down, but she ignored it.

"She's very pretty, and talented. I can see why you might like her. If you can ignore the bitchiness." She scrunched her face up in a snarl.

"Luna, you don't need to worry. I'm not interested in her. I'm mated to you. You're the one I want."

"Right. Because of the whole mate bond thing. I guess that's why I'm feeling so defensive."

My hand fell from her as she forced her arms to drop to her sides and blew a puff of air towards her forehead, ruffling her hair.

I put a hand on her cheek and turned her head so I could make eye contact. I wanted her to see the truth in my eyes. "That's not why I'm interested in you. It's because you're the most beautiful girl I've ever seen, and I love your fiery spirit, and how brave and strong you are. You amaze me."

Her eyes sparked with blue flames like I'd tossed on a log of driftwood, creating a new type of fire inside her. Suddenly, she pressed her lips against mine in a kiss that seared my skin. Fire exploded inside me and licked every inch of my body. I grabbed her around the waist and held on tight to her, letting the fire inside of me ravage her as hers consumed me.

We tumbled to the bed, tangled up together, when our legs threatened to disintegrate beneath us. She pawed at me, her nails raking at my shirt, tearing it open. A groan escaped both of us when her blazing hand pressed against my skin. I slipped my own hand under her shirt, and she writhed like my fingers were tongues of fire.

When I slid my hand inside the front of her jeans and pressed it against her, she cried out and pressed back. "Oh God, yes!"

Her words were a starter pistol, sending my desire racing, but she threw up a roadblock as soon as I took off. My body roared in protest, but when I saw the look on her face, I felt instantly guilty. Her eyes popped open, and her face twisted up as she dug her nails into my flesh. Tears squirted from the corners of her eyes. She shook her head and pushed me off her, sitting up.

"I'm sorry, Nikko. I shouldn't have started it. I'm so confused right now, I don't even understand what I'm feeling. Do I really want you, or is it just jealousy, fear, and the mate bond making me feel this way?" She wiped the tears from her agonized face.

I cautiously wrapped an arm around her. "It's okay, Luna. I understand. I'm here for you, whatever you need or want. But I don't want you to do anything you're not ready for."

She laid her head on my shoulder. Her chest heaved as she sobbed against me. Eventually, she whimpered, "I'm not as brave and strong as you think I am."

I stroked her back as I cradled her. "Yes, you are. Being brave doesn't mean you're never afraid, and being strong doesn't mean you never need help with anything."

She let me hold her for several minutes before she

lifted her head and sniffed back her tears, wiping her cheeks. "I think I need some sleep. I'm wiped out."

"Me too. I'll make up a bed on the floor." I moved to get up, but she reached for me.

"You can stay if you want." Her shaky voice and pleading eyes told me she wanted it, too.

Sleeping next to her but not touching her would be torture, but I wouldn't pass up the chance for the world. I took off my shirt and dropped my jeans to the floor, leaving on my boxer briefs, then pulled back the covers. Luna stared at me for a minute, biting her lip, then shimmied out of her own jeans.

"Do you want your pajamas?" I held out her duffel bag. She nodded and took it. I turned around, giving her a moment of privacy. When I turned back, her shirt and a pretty, blue bra lay on the floor, and she wore a tiny tee shirt that hugged her curves and a pair of flannel sleep pants.

She climbed under the covers, and I slid in beside her. After a moment of hesitation, I scooted closer, putting a hand on her hip. She nestled her backside up against me, and I forced my body to behave. I fell asleep with my face buried in her hair, her scent and warmth soothing me like a lullaby.

When I woke up in the morning, she'd rolled over and nuzzled against me, and my arm was holding her close. I wanted to stay that way forever, but she jerked awake a few minutes later and pushed herself away from me. I pretended I was just waking up, stretching and yawning.

"I need to use the bathroom." She grabbed her bag and moved towards the door, her face an emotionless mask. Did she regret being vulnerable with me last night? It was such a departure from her normal confidence, I should've expected it wouldn't last. Chipping away Luna's hard shell was going to be tougher than that.

I stayed in bed till she left since I had a massive hard-on. I waited a few minutes for her to get down the hall before grabbing my own bag and heading down to the men's room. I didn't think about the fact that I was wearing only underwear till Mara came out of the bathroom.

She made no effort to hide her curiosity as her eyes roved up and down my body. When they got back to my face, she quirked an eyebrow and said, "I thought Luna would take care of that for you."

I flapped my jaw like a fish, no clue how to respond to that. I was too stunned to even cover myself.

She smirked and turned into a doorway. "If you need some help, I'll be in my room."

I hurried past, rubbing one hand over my face and holding my bag in front of my crotch with the other. I slipped into the bathroom and groaned out loud when I realized it was empty.

After a cold shower, I went back to the room where Luna's scent bloomed from her warm, damp body as she brushed out her wet hair, reminding me of that day she'd first come into heat and her scent had grabbed ahold of me like a scythe and dragged me to her.

She wasn't in heat anymore, but her scent still called to me. I wanted to sidle up behind her and bury my face in her neck, breathe her in, but the look on her face told me she wouldn't respond to that the way I wanted her to.

I gave her a soft smile instead and said, "Ready for breakfast?"

She turned towards me and nodded. We walked in silence down to the dining room. I had no idea what was going through her head, but I was too afraid to say anything that might upset her.

A spread of food covered the table again, but only a few people were there at the moment. Unfortunately, one of them was Mara and another one was Cassius. They were cozied up next to each other. Mara scowled at Luna, but Cassius curled his lips in a smile.

I could sense Luna tensing beside me. I looped a hand through her arm in a silent promise to protect her. She didn't pull away from me, so I took it as sign that she didn't completely hate me, even though she was acting as cold and hard as stone.

Andor looked up when we came in and said, "Good morning. Help yourself to whatever you'd like. I promise it's all edible."

I grinned and escorted Luna to a seat as far away from Mara and Cassius as possible. We both filled our plates with breakfast meats, ignoring the bagels, muffins, and pastries. I would've preferred another steak, but I certainly wasn't going to complain. It was still hard to believe Andor had opened his doors and offered food and lodging to two strangers. He had to want something in return, but I had no idea what it was yet.

I didn't like feeling indebted to him, and I wanted to count the cost before I took too much of his charity, so I said, "I'm not a great chef, but I can cook a few things if you'd like us to take a turn making a meal. I want to do my part to help out."

"Thank you, Nikko. Yes, everyone shares the responsibilities of cooking, cleaning, and maintaining the property. We make up a schedule once a week, so we'll put you and Luna on the next one. In the meantime, feel free to relax and enjoy yourselves. I want this to be a refuge from the troubles of the outside world. There are televisions, a game room, computers, a pool, a workout room, and plenty of land for you to explore. Make yourself at home here."

I shook my head, blown away. This was like a fantasy world. I was free of the pressures of the pack and my dad's unattainable expectations, free from the prying eyes of the human world, and I had Luna here and all the time I wanted with her. "That sounds amazing. Thank you, Andor. I can't tell you how grateful we are."

Luna murmured her own heartfelt appreciation, and her face reflected almost the same sense of ease as mine. I dared to squeeze her hand under the table. "What would you like to do today, Luna?"

CHAPTER 19

NIKKO

"I want to work on shifting. I need to be able to control my wolf."

Of course she did. A normal girl might want to watch a movie or go for a swim, relax a little now that she was out of immediate danger, but it shouldn't have surprised me that Luna was more interested in training. I wasn't sure she would ever be able to relax and let her guard down. I made it my secondary goal, after winning her heart, to help her find peace. Maybe once she could control her wolf, she'd feel more in control of her life again.

"Okay, sure. I can help you work on that."

Cassius twisted his thin, red lips in a sly smile that looked like a bloody slash against his pale skin. "I can help, too. Provide a little extra motivation. She didn't seem to have any trouble shifting when I was around."

My eyes bulged in shock and rage, and my claws popped out, digging into the table. I didn't want that monster anywhere near her. I forced back the string of swear words that threatened to spew out at him and turned to Andor, expecting him to stand up for us. But instead, his face wrinkled up in a smile, and he nodded.

"That's very generous of you, Cassius. That's the kind of cooperation I like to see. Enemies learning to get along and help each other."

Mara didn't look too happy about it, but Cassius raised an eyebrow at me with a victorious smirk. "Shall we head to the lawn?"

I glanced out the window at the brilliant, pink and gold sunrise beaming over the top of the mountains. "It's daylight. Don't vampires have to stay out of the sun?"

"Most do, yes. But I'm lucky enough to have a witch friend who managed to put a ward around me. Makes life so much more convenient." He winked at Mara, ignoring the scowl she'd turned towards him, and gave another one of his signature, evil grins.

"Sounds good. Let's do it," Luna said before I had a chance to voice another protest.

She got up, leaving her plate for whoever had dish duty, then marched determinedly towards the front doors. I scurried after her, Cassius on my heels, breathing his hot stench down my neck. My skin puckered up with goosebumps.

Luna flung the doors open like she was on a mission and nothing would stop her from completing it. Light poured in, and I whipped around, hoping that the spell had failed and Cassius was burning up, but all it did was make his pale skin look even whiter and his slicked-back black hair shine like a raven's back. We trotted after Luna as she tromped out to the middle of the open lawn.

As soon as she got there, Cassius hurled himself at her with a snarl. His trim body flew through the air towards her like a streak of black lightning. My wolf reacted immediately, tearing out of me with a burst of energy that sent me leaping towards him. But Luna reacted just as quickly, her own body twisting and morphing as her bones cracked and black fur popped out of her skin. I jumped in between them, worried she wouldn't have the self-control to resist attacking him. Cassius stopped just short of us.

He shook his head, smiling and staring at us. If he was afraid of us, he didn't show it. "That was truly incredible. Such magnificent animals. I wonder how you would fare in a fight with me?"

I snapped my teeth and snarled at him, growling viciously. He held up his hands. "Just a thought."

I turned to Luna, grateful I could communicate with her telepathically so Cassius wouldn't hear. "I don't trust this guy, Luna. Let's tell him to get lost."

"No, he's good motivation. You said yourself, the more I practice, the easier it will be for me to control my shift. I want to do it again. I just have to figure out how to shift back."

My body heated, remembering how she managed to shift back last time, and the desires it inspired in her. "It's going to be hard to shift back when there's a threat around. Why don't we go somewhere private?"

"No, I have to learn to control my wolf, no matter what situation I'm in."

I had no idea how to help her calm down with a vampire looming beside her. I doubted I could even calm myself enough to shift back. It took all my self-control to keep my wolf from attacking.

Cassius quirked an eyebrow at us as we stared at each other. "What's happening here? Are you two communicating in some way?"

I growled and barked at him, communicating in a way he could understand, even if it wasn't English. He had the nerve to chuckle at me. My wolf fantasized about ripping his head off. That would shut him up.

As he spoke, his voice like melted dark chocolate, he gradually eased closer. "Let me guess. You're trying to help her shift back, but it's challenging because I'm here. But I'm not really a threat, now am I? I wouldn't actually hurt you. Besides, I'm just one, young vampire who's never fought a wolf before. And there are two of you. I'm sure you could easily take me down."

He carefully stretched out his palm towards Luna. Her body quivered, and her breath came in heavy pants. She sniffed his palm and whined but didn't snap at him, so he slowly turned his hand over and slid it up her snout then stroked the top of her head. A growl rumbled in the back of my throat, and my heart pounded, my body ready to lunge at him if he tried anything.

"Good girl. See? You're not in danger. Just relax." He kept stroking her fur then switched to scratching. She dipped and turned her head so he could reach behind her ear. Eventually, she laid down on the grass and put her head at his feet.

I let out a mournful howl of protest. What was going on here? Was she going to roll over and present her belly to him?

But before it went that far, Cassius took his hands off

her and stepped back. "Do you think you can shift back now?"

Luna chuffed. A few seconds later, she cried out as her body contorted back into its human form. She dropped to the ground with a thud, naked and breathing hard, but with a triumphant smile on her face. Then she jumped up and pumped her fists in a victory dance, heedless of her nudity. "I did it! I think I'm getting the hang of this."

Cassius took in an eyeful of her naked body, so I quickly moved in front of her, blocking his view and snarling at him.

"I want to try it again. This time, don't jump me, Cassius."

That wouldn't have been hard for me, since I still considered him a threat, but he'd tamed Luna's wolf so thoroughly, I doubted she would shift even if he did attack her. I offered some words of encouragement to help her out.

"Vampires are the enemy, Luna. You need to take down the threat. Let your wolf do what it was created to do."

Luna smirked at my ominous tone but then turned her attention to Cassius, staring him down with laser beam eyes.

"Come on, Luna. You can do it. Show me what you've got. I want to see that wolf again," he murmured seductively.

I chuffed at him. Did he really think that would work? But to my shock, it did.

Suddenly, Luna's wolf burst out again. She shook out her fur and gave a dopey grin. Cassius clapped and trotted over to her to scratch her under the chin. Her tongue hung out as he petted her. She shifted back a minute later.

"It's getting easier. Thanks, Cassius. You're a big help." She gave him that broad smile she'd only given me once and I'd been desperate to earn again.

I wanted to jump on him, tear him limb from limb, and rip his heart from his body. Since I couldn't do that, I wanted to bound off into the woods and burn off my frustration by racing through the trees in pursuit of something. But the last thing I wanted to do was leave Luna alone with him.

"No problem. Happy to help any time. How about a little fight, just to see what you've got?"

I couldn't help myself. A roar tore from my throat, and I lunged at Cassius, my sharp fangs aiming for his skinny neck. Luna's wolf exploded out of her, jumping between me and the vampire. I barely managed to stop myself from attacking her. She was protecting the vampire from me?

She growled and barked, snapping at me. "Nikko, no! You can't attack him! Calm down!"

I shook my body, trying to release some of the animalistic energy that was raring to be unleashed. "Are you insane? I could've killed you!"

"You were about to kill him! He didn't do anything!"

I looked around her and bared my teeth at him, growling. I didn't like how she had her back to him. He watched us with a smirk. "He wants to fight you. He'll tear you apart!"

"No he won't, Nikko. He's just trying to help. You're overreacting."

"We don't know anything about him, Luna! All we

know is he's a vampire. I know you're just a young pup and you don't know much about our kind, but vampires are our enemies. I don't care how much he sweet talks you or rubs your belly. He's dangerous! One bite could kill you. We shouldn't even be around him. Come on, let's go." I nipped at her neck, pulling her away from him.

She jerked away from me, snarling and snapping at me. "I'm not some stupid pup, Nikko! And you're not the boss of me. If I want to practice with him, that's my decision."

The alpha in me howled in protest. I wanted to demand her submission, but technically, I didn't have any authority over her since she wasn't in my pack.

"I forbid it! You're my mate, and you will obey me!" The words burst out before I could stop myself. I cringed at how much I sounded like my dad.

Luna's eyes narrowed and crystalized, hard as diamonds. "Is that what you expect? Well, keep dreaming! You're not my alpha, and I reject your claim on me!"

She howled at me and shifted back to her human form in a burst of rage, her fur flying. Then she turned to Cassius, arms crossed over her heaving chest. I shook with anger, expecting her to tell him she wanted to spar with him, but instead, she said, "I'm kind of tired and hungry. I think I need a break. But I'd love to work together some more later, if you want to."

"Sure, any time." Cassius glanced curiously between us but didn't ask what was going on. I'm sure he could figure it out.

Luna stomped away, tempting me to tear Cassius apart while I had the opportunity. Somehow, I managed to resist my baser instincts and loped away from him instead. I was too worked up to shift back, but I followed Luna towards the house.

When I got near enough to reach her, I nudged her flank. She stopped and whirled around to glare at me. "Don't touch me, Nikko. I don't want anything to do with you."

CHAPTER 20

LUNA

I SHIFTED BACK INTO A WOLF, THE TRANSITION EASY NOW. Or maybe it was just my rage making me want to wolf out. I bolted into the woods, away from Nikko, desperate to run and attack something. A deer spotted me and took off, so I chased after it.

With one leap I was on top of it, plunging my sharp fangs into its neck. It bleated out a final cry as blood gushed from its throat, spraying me. I gouged out a hunk of meat from its flank and swallowed it whole then tore out another and another in a wild frenzy. I was an animal. There was nothing human in me.

When my hunger and my thirst for blood was finally sated, I collapsed beside my kill, exhausted. Thick, congealing blood coated my paws, chest, and muzzle. I tried to wipe them clean on the forest foliage, but my fur was still sticky with it. I really was an animal.

At first, I hadn't wanted anything to do with being a wolf, but the more I let my wolf out, the more I realized it felt more natural than being human. There was no point denying it; I was a werewolf. And I needed a crash course in how to be one.

I hated that I'd had to run and hide instead of defending myself, but coming to the sanctuary was a good start. There, I could stretch my legs without worrying about being discovered. I didn't want to stay there forever, though. I missed my home and my family. I didn't want to give them up forever because of some stupid claim that Nikko had on me. But if I ever wanted to go home again, I'd have to fight for my freedom.

Just thinking about Nikko's demanding attitude made me want to fight with him. He'd been so nice lately, so gentle and caring, I thought I might actually be falling for him. I knew he was just trying to protect me, but I'd be damned if I was going to let him order me around. If that's what he expected from a mate, he could forget about it.

My thoughts drifted back to the conversation I'd overheard between my dad and my brother. Dad had implied that I was in line to be the alpha of our pack since I was the firstborn. No wonder I couldn't stand the thought of submitting to Nikko. I had alpha blood in me. Even once Bardolf was gone, there was no way I could mate with Nikko and live under his authority.

I couldn't let myself be swayed by his attempts to woo me. Even though he was cute, and could be sweet and kind, and we had incredible chemistry. I couldn't let myself forget that his goal was to get me to submit.

I had to learn how to fight so I could defend myself against him and all the other wolves that wanted me. What better sparring partner than a vampire? Despite Nikko's worries, I didn't think Cassius was a threat. Even if he hurt me, I could heal. And he'd be strong enough to withstand my attacks without me hurting him. It was the perfect opportunity.

I jumped up and headed back to the castle, intent on finding Cassius and taking him up on his offer to fight with me. I'd shredded my clothes, and I didn't want to go back to the room where Nikko probably was, so I stayed in wolf form, padding carefully around the castle, my nails clicking on the hardwood floors.

I followed Cassius' scent to the game room where I found him draped over Mara's back, leaning over the billiards table. His hands grasped her hips, adjusting her stance as she aimed a pool stick at the cue ball. Her black lace skirt was so short, only her tights kept me from seeing her ass cheeks. I'll admit, it was pure pettiness that led me to let out a bark to get their attention. I snickered when Mara scratched her stick across the felt and the ball skittered down the table.

She jerked upright, whipped her head around, and glared at me. "No dogs allowed inside, Fido."

Cassius dropped his hands from her hips and stepped towards me, smiling. "Hey Luna. Are you having trouble shifting? Need some help?"

Mara rolled her eyes at me.

I shook my head.

"Looking for Nikko?"

Another shake and a harsh chuff. I definitely was not looking for Nikko.

He quirked an eyebrow. "Did you want to spar now?"

I barked eagerly, and his soft smile spread wide, revealing sharp fangs. Not as big as mine, though.

Mara propped a hand on her hip and stomped her Doc

Marten as she flicked her flashing eyes between us. "Come on, we're in the middle of a game!"

"I promised Luna earlier that I would help her. And besides, we didn't even break yet. We'll play later." Cassius gestured to the undisturbed triangle of pool balls her last shot had completely missed.

I chuffed victoriously then trotted past her and out the doors that looked out over the back lawn. Cassius followed me. When I got to the center of the grassy space, I stopped. But Cassius looked around and wrinkled his face up.

"I got the feeling that Nikko didn't want you to do this."

I growled and barked, letting him know what I thought about Nikko's opinion.

"Maybe we should go somewhere else, where he can't see us."

He was right. Nikko would interfere if he saw us out here, and that would likely lead to trouble. He was so antagonistic towards Cassius, he might attack him for real. Who would win in a fight between them? I had no idea. Even if they both came out okay, Andor would probably kick us out of here.

But what Nikko didn't know wouldn't hurt him.

I barked and trotted off, searching for a secluded spot. But every side of the castle had windows overlooking it. After I'd made a full circuit around the castle and returned to where Cassius was at, he pointed off into the forest. "There's a clearing just beyond those trees. How about there?"

I chuffed and let him lead me through the small patch of woods, ignoring the tempting scent of prey in favor of a bigger prize. Sure enough, the trees gave way to a small, grassy meadow, sweet with the scent of wildflowers, just big enough for our needs. The sun shone down on it like a spotlight. With his dark hair and clothes and pale skin, Cassius looked out of place, like a ghost in broad daylight.

I should've expected it after last time, but it took me by surprise when, without warning, Cassius leapt towards me, his hands out like claws. Yelping, I reared up before he could gouge them into me. Then I crashed down on top of him, knocking him down. He hit the ground with a loud thud, like a boulder falling from the mountain.

For half a second, I worried that I had hurt him, until he shoved his hands into my chest with the force of a battering ram, tossing me off him. My body hurtled backwards, and I landed hard on my back, bruising my spine. I howled in pain and rolled around, regretting the whole idea of sparring. My first instinct to call it off, but if this was a real fight, I wouldn't give up that easily. And I needed to learn to defend myself.

A rush of adrenaline shot through me, spurring me into action. I forced myself to jump up. Cassius was waiting for me. He could've tackled me while I was down; he should've. A real opponent would have. I should've gotten up quicker instead of wallowing in pain. Next time I would.

I had to expect some pain and injury and be prepared to fight through it. Ignoring the ache in my back, I lunged towards Cassius with my fangs bared. He was obviously just as strong as me, if not stronger, so I had to work to my advantages. Number one being my powerful jaws filled with sharp fangs. I aimed for Cassius' neck, but he shoved his hands out again, holding me back. I barked and snapped at him.

Cassius bolted out from under me, then suddenly he was behind me. He launched himself onto my back, his hard-as-stone body slamming down onto my bruised spine. I yelped in agony as my back bowed. He wasn't showing me any mercy, but that was what I wanted.

Before I had a chance to recover from that pain, he wrapped his arms and legs around my flank and squeezed, his arms like a vise, tightening till my ribs started to crack. I felt the bones fracture with a loud crunch, the jagged shards piercing my insides. Instead of letting go, his grip only tightened, forcing the air out of my lungs, collapsing them. My body thrashed under him, trying to shake him off, but he held on tight. I jerked my head around, trying to bite him, but I couldn't reach.

I could drop to the ground, lay still in surrender. But at that point, I wasn't sure he'd stop even if I did. He had to realize how badly he was hurting me. Was he just trying to push me to my limit, leaving it up to me to call it off? Or was he so caught up in the fight he forgot it wasn't real?

I only had one option left. I knew it would hurt me just as much if not more than it hurt him, but I wasn't ready to give up yet. Clenching my muscles against the inevitable pain, I reared up and let myself fall backwards, crushing him under my back and sending spikes of pain into my spine. The sound of our fall echoed off the mountains and vibrated the ground around us.

I howled as my back broke with a horrifying snap. I couldn't move. I was paralyzed.

I let out a mournful cry of defeat and lay there,

motionless, as Cassius writhed out from under me. But even that wasn't enough to stop him. He pounced on my limp body, hammering it again, only this time I couldn't feel the pain, I could only hear the crunch of shattering bone.

He jerked his head back and ripped open his mouth, baring his glistening fangs. Was he going to bite me? My knowledge of vampires was limited to the questionable facts offered by movies and TV shows. Nikko had corroborated one of them. Their bite was lethal to werewolves.

I couldn't even push him away as he lunged at me.

CHAPTER 21

NIKKO

Her words echoed in my mind over and over again like a death knell, signaling the end of any relationship between us and declaring my failure. I'd made a fatal error, sealing my fate. Luna would never agree to be my mate now that I'd told her I expected her to obey me.

I was going to spend the rest of my life pining for a mate who rejected me. And I could never face my pack with that shame hanging over my head. I was destined to be alone forever.

I was just as worthless and pathetic as my father always said I was. Even my mate couldn't stand me, and she was bonded to me! Luna would rather be with a vampire than with me. And he was even better at helping her learn to control her wolf than I was!

But it wasn't just her submission I cared about, it was her safety. She didn't understand how dangerous Cassius was. She hadn't grown up hearing the legends about vampires and how deadly they could be. They were stronger, faster, and less susceptible to injury than we were. It could take a whole pack to bring one down.

Especially since one bite could kill. Once bitten, a werewolf's strong heart pumped the venom through his body in seconds, the poison searing his veins. There was no time to shift. The werewolf would writhe in agony then drop dead. It was a quick but horribly painful death.

Cassius was here because he couldn't control his impulses. I didn't care what his intentions were, I didn't want him anywhere near Luna. If he lost control for even a second, he could kill her.

Thank God she'd turned him down, at least for the moment. Maybe I could talk some sense into her after she cooled off. I would apologize and tell her I didn't want to control her, just protect her.

I doubted she'd believe that, but hopefully it would give me a chance to explain how dangerous vampires were. Even if she didn't want to be with me, I still felt the instinct to protect her. I was bonded to her, and that compulsion would never go away.

When she ran off into the woods, Cassius didn't follow her, so neither did I. Instead, I went inside to wallow in my inadequacies. Cassius headed for the game room, so I trudged upstairs to my room.

Luna's scent hung heavy in the air, a palpable reminder of what I'd lost. I choked on it, letting out a strangled cry. Then I threw myself onto the bed, burying my nose in her pillow, torturing myself some more. Those tender moments the night before were probably the last time I'd ever touch her. I squeezed her pillow to my chest, pretending it was her.

I laid there for a long time, desperate to fall sleep so I

could forget for a minute but unable to, until I heard what sounded like a bark coming from below me. Was that Luna? I listened closely for a minute, but I didn't hear another one. Maybe it was my imagination. I felt edgy, though, anxious to check on her.

I went downstairs, looking first in the dining room where the scent of pork chops tempted me to stay. But Luna wasn't in there, and neither was Cassius, only Jinx, who was magically popping in and out of the kitchen with platters of food.

"Jinx, have you seen Luna?"

"Yeah, she and Cassius are in the movie room watching Twilight and making out."

I snorted at first, but Jinx kept a straight face. Was Cassius really that into Luna? I raced out of the dining room and down the hall to the theater. When I heard the movie theme song, I hurled myself around the door. The movie was playing, but the room was empty.

Jinx appeared in front of the screen, his bell-like laugh ringing. "Gotcha!"

I clenched my fists and bared my teeth at him, growling. I would've rung his little fairy neck if I could've caught him, but he disappeared again. I didn't bother chasing after him.

Instead, I moved towards the game room where I'd last seen Cassius headed. But Mara was alone in there, shooting pool. She looked up when I stomped into the doorway.

"Have you seen Luna?"

She pursed her lips in a pout. "Yeah, she and Cassius went off together. But I'm free if you're looking for company. Wanna play pool with me?"

After Jinx's prank, I didn't know if I could believe her, but my nerves had ratcheted up, and I could smell a lingering trace of Luna's scent. I needed to find her and make sure she was safe. "Where did they go?"

Mara frowned at me but pointed towards the door. "Out back."

My heart took off like a race horse, pounding down the track, and my legs followed suit, propelling me out the door. I didn't see anyone on the back lawn, so I let my wolf out and dashed around the castle, stalking a trail of Luna's scent. It circled all the way around then headed towards the trees.

When I heard a yelp of pain coming from that direction, I took off towards it. Thunderous sounds echoed around me, like an avalanche, but I didn't see any rocks falling from the mountains in the distance. Another yelp spurred me on. I surged through the woods, weaving between the trees, going so fast I was bound to slam into one sooner or later. But I couldn't worry about my own safety, not when Luna's was in jeopardy.

One more crashing sound, then a howl I could recognize anywhere, only it sounded more tortured than I'd ever heard before. The high-pitched noise shattered my heart like glass. Was she dead? Had he killed her? But a mournful cry gave me hope that there was still time to save her.

I burst through the trees into a bright meadow. The sun blinded me for a moment, but then my eyes zeroed in on a black lump. I struggled to make sense out of what I was seeing at first, but then I realized Luna was on the ground, and Cassius was on top of her. He reared his head back and bared his fangs, ready to bite her.

Concentrating every ounce of strength and will into my legs, I leapt towards them. My body shot forward like a spring, arching over a greater distance than I'd ever jumped before. I was flying. I landed on Cassius' back with a loud grunt, knocking him off Luna.

He tumbled and so did I, somersaulting over him. I immediately righted myself and lunged for him again before he could get to Luna. But he wasn't heading for her, he was coming for me.

He bared his fangs and hissed as he leapt at me. I reared up onto my hind legs so he couldn't get his arms around my neck. I knew he was probably stronger than me, so I had to be smarter.

I came down with my mouth open, biting onto his arm. He shrieked as I lifted him off the ground and shook him back and forth. I wanted to tear his arm out of its socket, but his body was hard as stone. Too bad my bite wasn't poisonous.

I glanced at Luna, expecting her to come hurtling towards me, either to help me or defend Cassius, I wasn't sure. But she hadn't moved. She still lay on the ground, lifeless. Was she already dead? Grief crashed into me, and my body stumbled backwards.

Cassius took the opportunity to swing his other arm towards me. He raked his diamond hard nails across my flank, tearing deep gouges. I howled in pain as I flung him to the ground, but I didn't let my injury stop me. My life didn't matter anymore, only my vengeance. There was no one more ruthless than a wolf seeking to avenge his lost mate.

I immediately pounced on him and clamped my jaws around his neck. He pummeled his hands into my chest like a jackhammer, each blow cracking a rib, but I ignored the pain and clenched my jaw tighter around his throat. His flesh shrieked like tearing metal as I tried to rip off his head.

But then he managed to get his hands around my own neck. He squeezed hard, choking me, trying to loosen my jaws. My hot saliva dripped onto his face. I didn't know if I had the strength to finish him off before he killed me, but I would die trying.

Suddenly, a loud cry wretched from Luna's throat. My jaw loosened in shock and I whipped my head towards her. She wasn't dead! Her wolf contorted with the crack of breaking bones and morphed back into a human.

Cassius took advantage of my distraction and tossed me off him. I tumbled as I hit the ground. Then he hurled himself towards me, his fangs bared. But he was coming too fast; I couldn't respond quick enough.

He slammed into my flank, his nails gouging into my side. I yelped and flailed and whipped my head towards him, snapping my jaws at his head and hands, but I couldn't get my mouth around him before he flung himself onto my back and started to squeeze my neck.

I shook my body, trying to knock him loose, but his hold was too strong. I was helpless. I heard him hiss as he opened his mouth, ready to bite.

Suddenly, something crashed into us, knocking us both over. Luna! She'd morphed back into a wolf.

When Cassius hit the ground, she pounced towards him. Her mouth immediately clamped around his head. She shook her head, trying to tear his off, but it stayed attached as his body flopped and jerked. I jumped on top of him, holding down his body, then latched my own mouth around his throat. My fangs broke through his stone-like skin, cracking it.

With a loud crack like shattering stone, Luna ripped his head off and tossed it away from his body. It hit the ground and rolled, landing face up a few yards away from us, the dark eyes lifeless. Cassius' body went still.

Luna let out a howl loud enough to shake the mountains then dropped to her belly and buried her snout in her paws. I padded over to her and rubbed my flank along hers then laid down next to her and nuzzled her with my snout. I could feel her heart pounding hard and fast against me. She whimpered and nuzzled me back.

I didn't say anything, just comforted her. This wasn't the time for I-told-you-so's or how-could-you's. I didn't care that I'd been proven right, all I cared about was that she was safe now. But she was man enough to admit her mistake.

"I'm sorry I didn't listen to you. You were right. He would've killed me if you hadn't shown up. Thank you for saving me. I'm surprised you did after what I said to you."

I jerked my head up so I could look into her eyes. "Luna, I consider you my mate, whether you do or not, and I will do everything in my power to protect you. I'm sorry I acted like I did earlier. I don't expect you to obey me. You're strong, and smart, and I know you can take care of yourself most of the time. I just want to keep you safe."

She sighed and pushed her head against mine. "I wish things were different. If we didn't have to worry about packs and alphas and all that..."

Hope bloomed in my chest. Was she saying what I

thought she was? "I think we make a pretty good team, don't you? We took down that vampire together."

She chuffed and smiled, but then it dropped into a frown. "Do you think Andor will kick us out when he finds out what happened? We don't have any proof that Cassius tried to kill us."

"He might. He doesn't know us, and he obviously trusted Cassius. What do you want to do if he does?" I clenched my body and held my breath, waiting for her answer.

She didn't get a chance to tell me, though, before another wolf burst through the nearby trees.

CHAPTER 22

LUNA

"Zander!" I jumped up in disbelief when my brother came bounding out of the woods towards us, his dark brown fur glossy in the sunlight. I'd only seen his wolf in the dark before, but I recognized his smell immediately. The familiar scent brought a rush of homesickness.

He skidded to a halt then whipped his head back and forth in confusion between me, Nikko, and Cassius' body. Then he leapt in between Nikko and me, barking and snarling and snapping his jaws at him. "What are you doing here? Get away from my sister!"

Nikko barked and growled at my brother, his claws raking the ground. The two made moves like they were about to jump each other.

"Stop, both of you!" I pushed in between them, hoping they wouldn't attack me by accident.

Zander flicked his eyes up and down my flank. Since I'd shifted, there was no evidence of the mortal wounds Cassius had inflicted. "Did he hurt you, Luna?"

"No, I'm fine. He… saved me." I tilted my head towards Cassius' body.

Zander backed up and went over to investigate. His fur stood up and his body tensed when he got a good whiff of him. "Is that a… vampire?"

"Yeah, he tried to bite me, but we killed him. He was one of the residents at the sanctuary."

Zander nudged the lifeless body with his snout and jumped back like he was worried it would reanimate. Then he padded over to Cassius' head and pawed at it. When he was convinced that Cassius was no longer a threat, he trotted back over towards me. He kept his espresso eyes narrowed on Nikko but didn't try to attack him.

"So you found the sanctuary?"

"Yeah, it's amazing."

"Who else lives there? Any of the other residents dangerous?"

I snorted out a laugh. He wouldn't believe me if I told him all the creatures that lived there. It was almost too much for me to believe. Instead, I just said, "I'm okay."

"Why is he here? Did he kidnap you?" He glared at Nikko who growled under his breath. I could feel Nikko's body coursing with adrenaline, ready to attack, his silvery fur quivering.

I shook my head vigorously. "No! He saw me leaving town and followed me. He thought if he left, too, his dad wouldn't have any cause to fight ours. He's been taking care of me."

Zander snorted. "Is that what he calls claiming you against your will?"

There was no point trying to convince him otherwise;

I knew he couldn't see Nikko as anything but an enemy. But he hadn't gotten to know him like I had. I decided to change the subject instead.

"Why are you here, Zander?"

"I was supposed to come with you, remember? But you ditched me. When Dad found out that Nikko disappeared at the same time, he worried that he'd taken you. He sent me to find you."

I could feel the tension radiating off him. I rubbed my flank against his and nudged my snout into his neck. "I'm sorry I left you, but I didn't want you to have to give up your life for me. And I knew Dad would need you if Bardolf's pack decided to attack. What's going on back home?"

Zander growled and started pacing, his dark fur quivering. "When Nikko disappeared, Bardolf went nuts. He showed up for the fight acting like a raving lunatic, claiming our pack had taken his son. He wanted to start a pack war right then."

I gasped and let out a distressed howl. Nikko immediately ran his body against my flank and nudged his head under mine. Zander stared at us.

"Did they?" I choked out.

Zander shook his head. "Dad told them that our pack hadn't touched Nikko, but that you had disappeared, too, and suggested maybe Nikko had taken you. Bardolf didn't care. He still wanted his pack to attack, but they resisted. All of us were there in our wolf form, and they could see we were stronger than they thought. Bardolf tried to command them to fight, but they stood up to him. They said there was no justification."

I didn't recognize the momentousness of that, but the

way Nikko reacted, I could tell it was a big deal. He let out several loud howls and clawed at the ground anxiously.

Zander waited for Nikko to settle down some before continuing. "It gets worse. Bardolf attacked several of his own pack and killed them before the rest of the pack ran off. I don't know what's happening there now. That's when Dad sent me to look for you."

It sounded to me like Dad was trying to get Zander out of there to protect him. I turned to Nikko, who was frozen. "What do you think is going on in your pack?"

"If the pack is resisting my Dad's orders, he won't let that go. He'll kill anyone who disobeys him. Eventually, the pack will give in, and they will attack your pack. Lots of lives will be lost on both sides. I have to go back there, Luna. I have to stop this." His voice was resolute even though his body was shaking with fear.

"How are you going to stop it?"

"I'll fight my father, try to take him down."

"Do you think you can?"

"I don't know. He's stronger than me, but I'm younger, faster. I have more stamina. Maybe I can wear him down." He didn't sound very confident about it.

The thought of Nikko dying at his own father's hand hit me in the gut like a stab wound. All of this had started because of me. He didn't deserve to die for me. If he was brave enough to sacrifice his life, I needed to be, too.

I took a deep breath, puffed up my chest, and said, "I'll go with you. I'll submit to your claim if that will bring an end to this."

Zander howled in protest then rushed towards me, barking, his fur flying. "Luna, no! You're betraying our pack and our family. He's the enemy!"

I blocked Nikko's body with my own, sure that Zander was going to attack him. "No he's not, Zander. He's nothing like his father."

I thought Nikko would be thrilled, or at least relieved, but instead, he shook his head, his amber eyes as hard as the stone they resembled. "I wish it would, but it's not even about that anymore. He just wants a reason to fight. It was wrong of me to claim you against your will. I don't want to take your life from you. I release you from my claim. You're free."

That little word hit me like a wrecking ball, knocking the wind out of me and putting a hole in my chest. It was what I'd wanted, so why did my body feel like it was dying? I was still trying to process it when Nikko continued.

"My father isn't fit to be an alpha; alphas don't attack their own pack. Someone needs to take him down. I won't be able to live with myself if I let my dad attack your pack and kill your family. The odds are, I won't be able to stop him, but I have to try."

Nikko started walking away like he was leaving right then. In a panic, I scurried after him. "Wait! What about his beta?"

"He's too loyal to my father. He'd never oppose him. Since I'm next in line, it's my responsibility. It has to be me."

He stared at me for one long moment, emotions swirling in his eyes. "Goodbye, Luna." Then he took off again, running this time, back towards his pack, leaving me behind as he resolutely headed for his destiny. He didn't promise to come back to me or even say he'd see me again, probably because he knew he wouldn't make it.

My body shook with fear, and my fur stood up, crackling with electricity. I thought my heart would pound right out of my chest. My mouth went dry, parched. I was stranded in a desert, and there was nothingness for miles around. I was all alone.

As soon as Nikko's wolf crested over the horizon, out of sight, I snapped out of my shock. With a strangled cry, I raced after him. I couldn't let him die without telling him how I felt about him.

But Zander chased after me and nipped at my flank. "Luna, stop! You can't go back. It's not safe for you. If Nikko can't take down his father, there's going to be a war. You're just a pup; you don't know how to fight. You'll get killed, or worse, taken."

My hackles raised in defense at the insult. I wanted to deny it, insist that I could hold my own. But his ominous warning slowed me down some. "What do you mean, taken?"

Zander jumped in front of me, blocking the path, and elaborated. "Since Nikko released his claim on you, you're fair game for anyone else. They'll start a war just trying to claim you."

A shiver of revulsion rolled through me. I couldn't stand the thought of being claimed by anyone else, especially now that I realized I wanted to be with Nikko.

"Stay here, and I'll come back for you when it's safe." He tried to sound confident, but I could see the fear in his eyes. Fear that it would never be safe for me. Fear that he'd never see me again.

But like Nikko, he didn't linger for a long, heartfelt goodbye. Instead, he loped off after him, his own war to wage.

I stood, staring after them, feeling helpless, like my whole life, my entire world, was up in the air, out of my control. All I could do was wait to see what remained when the dust settled. But the odds were, everything I cared about would be gone.

There was no way I was going to stay there, hidden away in the mountains, while others decided my fate. I'd rather die trying to protect the people I cared about than live with the regret that I could've done more. But discretion was the better part of valor, so rather than barreling into town like a crusader, I decided to keep my return a secret until I needed to reveal myself.

I bounded off in the direction of home, abandoning the few personal possessions I'd brought with me. They weren't worth risking Andor's judgement. In wolf form, the journey through the mountains was no challenge at all. When I reached my truck, I realized I didn't have my keys, but I didn't need them, or the vehicle. I could travel almost as fast on four paws. Maybe even faster since I could take a direct route. I had no map, but my wolf sensed the direction of home like a migratory bird.

I loped into town at sunset. A pink, blue, and purple sky painted the backdrop, making the shadowy outline of my house the subject of a picturesque scene. I'd always been eager to grow up and go off on my own adventures, but now the familiar comfort of home wrapped around me. I could do something extraordinary right here. And I might have to if I wanted a home to return to.

CHAPTER 23

NIKKO

I MADE THE TRIP HOME IN A QUARTER OF THE TIME THAT IT took Luna and me to get to the sanctuary, but without her, the trip felt like a march to the gallows. I kept her face in the back of my mind as motivation, something to live for. Maybe when it was all over, if I survived, I might have another chance to win her. But it would take a lot more than the will to survive if I was going to come out of this victorious.

Those words I'd longed to hear from her echoed in my mind. She was willing to accept my claim to prevent a pack war. It killed me to turn her down. But I couldn't let my own desires cloud my judgement. I had to do what was right for everyone, not just for me.

I was exhausted from a long, stressful day. All I wanted to do was crawl in my own bed and sleep for a good ten hours. But I knew if I went inside, I'd have my father to answer to. It was easier to sleep out in the woods beside the house where I could keep an eye on any comings or goings. I found an off-the-path spot where I could curl up on a bed of pine needles. Despite the worries bouncing around in my head, sleep claimed me quickly.

When I woke in the morning, I felt physically renewed if not mentally. But I was clear-headed enough to know that I couldn't approach my father at home to tell him I wanted to challenge him. I hated to think it, but knowing my father, he might try to take me down right then, with no witnesses and no rules. As far as anyone knew, I had already disappeared. It would be easy for him to make me disappear forever.

Instead, I shook the dew off my fur and headed to my friend Roane's house. I didn't know what time it was, but the position of the sun, still hovering just above the orange horizon, gave me hope that I might be able to catch him before he went to school. Sure enough, his truck sat in the driveway when I arrived. I jumped in the bed to wait for him. When he came out a few minutes later, I popped up.

He jerked in surprise, his face going from stressed to shocked to happiness, all in a moment. "Nikko! Where have you been, man? Your dad's been going crazy!"

I couldn't talk to him while I was a wolf and he was human, so I quickly shifted. "I know. I heard the gist of it. I came back to stop him. I'm going to challenge his position as alpha."

Roane's eyes widened till his irises looked like small, bronze buttons floating in the whites. "Are you nuts? There's no way you can beat your father, but if you challenge him, you'll have to fight to the death!"

I scowled at him. So much for my support system. He was right, of course, but it would've been nice if one person could've had faith in me. "I know. But what am I supposed to do? Stand by and let him attack the Ammon pack? Then we'll all have to fight, and a lot more of us will die. My father has lost control; someone has to stop him."

He shook his head, his happy face turning somber again. "Bro, I thought you were gone for good. I already mourned you once. You gonna make me do it again? You're gonna be dead for sure if you do that. Then what'll happen? If you think your father's acting crazy with you missing, what's he's gonna be like when you're dead at his own hand? He's gonna go berserk."

Guilt weighed down on me, making me feel trapped. There was no way to escape it, no matter what I did. But the guilt I'd feel if I didn't try to stop this would be much worse than if I tried and failed.

"Maybe, but I have to try. I can't let him attack Luna's family. Will you go with me as a witness when I challenge him?" I didn't have to explain my request. Roane had known my dad his whole life. He knew what he was like, and what he was capable of.

He swallowed down his argument and nodded. "Of course. Why don't we get the guys, and we'll all go?"

"The more witnesses, the better."

Roane went inside and got some clothes for me to wear—sweatpants with a drawstring I could tighten and his smallest tee shirt. They still hung on me. Roane was massive, but so was my dad. All I could think about were all those hours he spent pumping iron and telling me I should do the same. I wished I'd listened to him about that. He was probably going to tear me apart before I even got a swipe in.

We drove to the school, since that's where most of my friends would be. I didn't even have to round them up.

When they saw me get out of Roane's truck, they immediately surrounded me with a barrage of questions. But they all got quiet real fast when I told them what I was planning. None of them were bold enough to tell me I was nuts like Roane had, but I could see it in the way they tensed up and their eyes shifted back and forth between each other. But like loyal pack members, they had my back.

Thirty minutes later, the word had spread from them, to their families, to everyone in the pack. When Roane and I pulled up in front of my house, the entire pack had congregated on the lawn in wolf form, shuffling around, whining, and letting off anxious howls as they waited for my arrival. I could smell their anxiety in the air like a pungent musk. My dad stood on the porch, bulging arms crossed over his broad chest and his tree trunk legs in a wide stance as he stared me down. I could feel the malice in his gaze like a laser target on an assault rifle, aimed right at me.

I yanked off Roane's oversized clothes as soon as I got out of the truck then shifted so the pack could all hear me. My father shifted, too, then climbed down the stairs, his giant, silver wolf even larger than I remembered. The pack cleared a path between us. We came face to face in front of them, although, my father's wolf towered over me like a statue, hard as steel, so I had to look up to meet his glinting eyes.

I didn't give him a chance to talk. I knew he'd only intimidate me, and no matter what I said, he'd make me look stupid. The less talking, the better. Instead, I tried to control the shivers that shot through my body like jolts of electricity as I forced myself to maintain eye contact.

"Bardolf Brisbane, I challenge you for the position of pack alpha."

Barks and howls echoed around us as I confirmed the rumor that had spread like a wildfire and brought them all to my doorstep to witness my challenge.

My father chuffed at me. "You think you can beat me, boy? Look at you, you're just a puppy. You really want to die today, right here, right now?"

I had assumed the fight would take place another time, after we'd both had a chance to prepare. But no matter what I did, my chances wouldn't improve much. There was no point putting it off. If I didn't do this now, I might lose my nerve.

I gulped and lifted my head higher. "I'm willing to take that risk."

"Well, we might as well do this, then, since everybody's already here." He stepped closer and growled at me, still trying to intimidate me. But I'd already made my challenge. There was no going back. I stared at him in silent agreement.

He wasn't broadcasting any of his thoughts, so I wasn't sure what was going on in his head. I couldn't imagine he'd be okay with the idea of fighting his own son to the death, but his only other option was to voluntarily concede. I knew he would never be willing to do that, even if it meant he had to kill me. It confirmed what I'd known all along but didn't want to believe—my father loved power more than he loved me.

When I didn't back down from his stare, he whipped himself around to address the pack, his thoughts strong and unwavering like it meant nothing to him at all. "My son has challenged me as pack alpha. I will defend my authority here today in front of all of you. Let us prepare the ring."

The pack responded with howls as they took off into the woods. They returned one by one with rocks in their mouths that they formed into a large circle in the center of the lawn. When the circle was complete, the pack surrounded it, leaving an opening for my father and me to enter the circle.

I forced my quaking body forward, into the ring, then moved to one side of it. My father took the other side. The pack surrounded the circle, their own bodies quivering with anticipation. I knew many of them agreed with me, that my father was not fit to serve as alpha any longer, and were rooting for me to win. But they would do nothing to help me defeat him. The challenge was mine alone. None of them would even vocalize their support for me, in fear of retaliation should my father win.

Roane stood on one side of the circle, his eyes alone telling me he supported me. His father, Gunnolf, was on the other side. Did he really think my father was a good alpha, or was he just too loyal to oppose him? If I made it out alive, as the new alpha, I would have the power, and the responsibility, to kick out any pack members who wouldn't concede to my authority. Would my dad's beta submit to me? Regardless, there would be a huge shift in the distribution of power among the pack.

I couldn't worry about those things now, though. I had a fight to win first. And the odds were, I was the only one who'd be gone tomorrow.

With a mighty roar, Gunnolf howled, "Let the challenge begin!"

My father didn't give me even a moment's advantage.

He hurled himself at me with a loud growl, teeth bared and claws extended. I rose up on my hind legs so he wouldn't land on top of me and threw myself at him.

My claws sank into his back, tearing through the fur and flesh. He tossed me off him like a pesky housefly, ripping my claws loose. Blood seeped out, leaving red streaks on his silvery fur. The pack howled, most of them in surprise. I wanted to take pride in making the first mark, but I couldn't bring myself to celebrate wounding my own father.

I landed hard on my back. I immediately tried to right myself, but my father pounced on me, digging his own claws into my belly. Pain radiated from each gouge. I tried to block it out and whipped my head back and forth, keeping away from his sharp teeth as his powerful jaws snapped at my face. All it would take was one bite to my neck, and he'd tear out my throat. The fight would be over.

I wasn't ready to lose that quickly. I had to get off the ground. With a surge of adrenaline, I leapt up, throwing him off me. He quickly rolled over then jumped back up. I thought it would take him a second to recover, but without a pause, he lunged at me, coming at me from the side.

His massive body rammed into me, knocking me over, almost to the edge of the circle. The wolves backed up to give us more room. At the same time, his jaws latched onto the side of my neck. I couldn't shake him loose, my efforts only made his jaw tighten, but I scrambled to keep him from getting on top of me, at least. He raked at my face with his paw, shredding the skin on my snout, as he tried to tear a chunk of flesh from my neck. I barely shut my eyes in time to prevent them being scratched out.

I was trapped. In that position, I could do nothing to him. I couldn't even defend myself. There was only one thing I could do. Taking a deep breath and clenching my muscles against the pain, I threw my weight in the opposite direction at the same time he yanked backwards. His teeth ripped through my neck, tearing it open, and he took a hunk of it with him as we separated.

I howled in agony and stumbled backwards, off balance. My vision blurred. I could feel every heartbeat as blood gushed from the wound, coating my fur in a wash of red. Another chorus of barks and howls rose up around us. The world started to go black, and I was tempted to let myself fade into the darkness, but Luna's face appeared in my mind. I had to protect her. I forced my eyes open and tried to focus on my father.

I knew he wouldn't give me any time to recover, and I was right. He pounced on me, aiming straight for my throat again. His teeth sank deep into the open wound, hitting a nerve that dropped me to my belly.

I yelped and whimpered. I knew I had to tear myself free before he bit all the way through my neck, but I couldn't bring myself to do it. In that moment of hesitation, he jumped onto my back, the heavy weight of him pressing me into the ground. Now there was no way I could get out of his grip. All he had to do was finish me.

Before he did, though, a commotion stirred up in the pack around us. I couldn't turn my head to see what was happening, and my dad was smart enough not to, either. He held on, biting at my neck.

Suddenly, a loud ruckus rose up from the crowd, and

another weight slammed into me as someone jumped onto my father. The force knocked him off me. I scrambled to my feet and whipped around to see what was happening. No one was allowed to interfere in a challenge.

But the person in the ring with us didn't know enough about our kind to know that.

CHAPTER 24

NIKKO

I STARED IN AWE AS LUNA LUNGED FOR MY FATHER, FEAR and admiration warring in my mind. Her presence alone was such a surprise, she managed to get a swipe in before my father barreled into her. I didn't hesitate. There was no way I was letting him hurt her.

I bounded towards them, latching onto my father's neck while Luna distracted him. He yelped and whipped his head towards me, snapping, and Luna took the opportunity to jump on him. His massive body hit the ground with a thunderous boom. Luna clamped down on the back of his neck, forcing his head to the ground.

He was much more powerful than her, so we only had a second before he would manage to throw her off, but that was all I needed. With a roar, I ripped my teeth from his neck, leaving deep gouges. He howled in pain, but I forced myself to ignore it. I couldn't afford to show him any mercy. He had none for me.

Then I lunged for him again, this time wrapping my

jaw almost all the way around his neck. With one powerful bite, I severed his jugular. His blood spurted into my mouth, hot and metallic. I let it coat my mouth as I bit at his throat again, trying to separate his head from his body. It was the only way I'd be convinced that the fight was over.

When his head tore free, his eyes rolled backwards, and his tongue flopped from the side of his mouth. His body went limp under Luna as his last breath squeezed out of his lungs. The pack howled out in a raucous melee at the sight of their fallen leader.

I slumped to the ground, overwhelmed. I'd done it! I'd taken down my father and won the role of alpha. I'd saved Luna's family. But now it was all up to me to lead this pack. A heavy sense of inferiority weighed me down. How could I ever succeed as alpha if I hadn't even been able to take my father on my own?

Luna got up and padded over to me then laid down beside me. Nothing she could've said would help me accept the fact that I'd just killed my own father, but she didn't say anything. She just started licking the wound on my neck. When it was clean, she moved to my muzzle, bathing my ragged snout with her warm, wet tongue. I laid my head on the ground and closed my eyes as she worked.

When she was finished, I opened my eyes and turned my head to look at her. "Thank you, Luna. I couldn't have done it without you."

She let her mouth hang open in a wolfy smile. "Didn't you tell me we make a great team?"

I chuckled at her, but then her expression grew serious.

"You're my mate. I didn't want you to have to do this alone, and I didn't want to risk losing you."

Her words inflated my chest with hope, and I rose up on my haunches. Did that mean she wanted to be with me? I couldn't believe it. "I released my claim on you, Luna. You're not bound to me anymore."

Her blue eyes stared into mine, as wide and clear as the sky. "What if I still want to be?"

I couldn't help myself. I launched myself at her, licking and nipping at her snout, my tail wagging so hard I thought it might tear itself right off my backside. She gave back as good as she got, and soon we were rolling on the ground together.

Roane's bellowing voice broke up the celebration. "Alright, already, Alpha Nikko! Think you can finish that later? You've got a pack to command."

I pulled away from Luna with a goofy grin, too happy to be embarrassed. Then I stood up and addressed the pack who were milling about, anxiously awaiting my first orders. A minute before, I felt terrified and overwhelmed by the responsibility, but now, with Luna at my side, I knew I could handle it.

"As the winner of this battle, I claim the position of alpha. But my mate, Luna, has alpha blood, too. I couldn't have won this challenge without her, and I don't want to lead this pack without her, either. We will lead this pack together, as co-alphas."

She gawked at me, but I smiled at her and nudged her flank. Luna was made to be an alpha, even more so than me. I wouldn't take that right from her. Together, we would be better than I could ever be on my own.

A hum rose up among the pack. No one could fathom

the idea of two alphas, let alone a female one. But none of them had ever met a she-wolf, either. Luna was special in every way possible.

I didn't give them a chance to speak up, though, or even process the statement before I moved on. That wasn't the only major change I was making.

"We are not going to rule like my father did, at war with our neighbors. Under our rule, this pack will no longer be at enmity with the Ammon pack. We were once one pack, and they are our brothers."

That garnered another loud reaction. It seemed mostly positive, but I didn't want to start my rule with a pack full of dissenters, so, feeling brave, I offered them an unprecedented choice, one that could possibly create a whole new set of enemies for me.

"If you don't want to live under my rule, I'll give you one chance to leave. Go now, and there will be no retaliation."

The pack grew eerily silent as sons, fathers, and brothers looked around at each other nervously. I held my breath, waiting to see if anyone would leave. I glanced at Gunnolf, who stared at his son with a tortured look on his face. Did I dare trust him? He'd always been completely loyal to my father. But I didn't want to lose Roane, and I couldn't bring myself to make him choose between me and his dad.

"Gunnolf, you're welcome to stay, but not as my beta. That position will go to your son. Can you live with that?"

Gunnolf gave a stiff, small nod, and he, Roane, and I all let out a collective breath.

When I looked back out at the pack, no one else had

budged. My father had taught me to never show weakness, not even in the form of joy, but I couldn't hold back my smile. I was nothing like my father, but that didn't mean I couldn't be a good alpha. In fact, I believed it would make me a better one.

CHAPTER 25

LUNA

I'd never felt more nervous in my life, and that was saying a lot coming from someone who'd turned into a werewolf, killed a vampire, fought the most powerful alpha, and narrowly avoided a pack war.

Nikko saw me tugging at the clothes he'd given me with a pained look twisting my face. "Are you sure, Luna? I don't want you to feel forced into this."

Did he really think he could force me into anything? Now that I understood my bossy, domineering nature was a product of my alpha blood and not a personality flaw, I was owning it. I wasn't born to be submissive.

I wanted to roll my eyes at him, but instead, I unclenched my hands, smoothed the wrinkles I'd put in the shirt, then forced my grimace into a smile. "This is what I want, Nikko. It's my decision, and they'll just have to live with it."

Delaying it wouldn't make the confrontation any easier, so I stiffened my back and headed towards the door. Nikko followed behind me. He was probably just as nervous as I was, heading into enemy territory to stake his claim.

We climbed into Nikko's truck and made the drive to my parents' house, the silence between us only ratcheting up the tension. We were both lost in our thoughts. It felt like a world away, but we were there way too soon.

Dad's truck sat in the driveway, confirming my assumption that he'd be home, even though he should've been at work by now. I was sure he was gearing up for a pack war. At least I could give him some good news.

But my heart sank when I saw that my mother's car was missing. Had my father sent her off somewhere to protect her? Would I ever see her again? It all depended on how my father reacted.

Nikko squeezed my hand as he turned off the engine then looked at me with a pained smile. He didn't offer any words of encouragement, probably because he couldn't think of any. We both knew this was not going to go well.

My dad must've heard Nikko's truck pull into the driveway, because he came outside to see who was there. My brother stepped out behind him. I couldn't decide if it was better or worse to have them both there for this.

When my dad saw Nikko, his body tensed and bristled like his wolf was about to explode out of him. He tore his gaze away from Nikko when I hurried over to him, my arms outstretched.

"Luna, are you okay?" He hugged me tight then pulled me away enough that he could look at me and stroke my hair.

I kept my arms wrapped around his waist, though, savoring the musky scent and the strong feel of him under his flannel shirt. I didn't want to let go of him in case this was the last time I saw him. Just because Nikko had declared an end to the rift between the packs didn't mean my father would agree to it. Joining Nikko's pack might still mean giving up my family.

"I told you to stay at the sanctuary till I came for you," Zander grumbled.

"I'm fine. Everything's okay now."

Dad's eyes shifted back towards Nikko, hard and glinting. "What's he doing here?"

Nikko stepped forward. "My father is dead, and I've taken his place as alpha. I'd like to make a truce with you."

Dad and Zander gawked at Nikko then at each other, rendered speechless for a long moment. I could see my dad's body relax as the tension fell off him. Eventually, Zander said, "You managed to take him down?"

Nikko glanced at me, his jaw tight. I nodded encouragingly. "With Luna's help, yes."

Dad and Zander shifted their stunned looks towards me. Dad's face rumpled up in worry, even though it was obvious I'd survived. "Luna? You fought against Bardolf? What were you thinking?"

"She's amazing, Lupin. So brave. She killed a vampire, too." Nikko stared at me with so much adoration, I knew I had to be brave enough to stand up for him, too.

"I didn't want Nikko to die, trying to protect us from his father. I…I love him."

I reached out and laced my fingers with Nikko's, staring down at our joined hands. When I looked up, Dad and Zander were staring at them, too. Their faces hardened.

"He's using you, Luna. He claimed you against your will. He took advantage of your ignorance." Dad frowned at me like he thought I was still too ignorant to understand.

I held tight to Nikko's hand and looked my father in the eye. "But then he gave up his family and his pack for me. He kept me safe and taught me how to control my wolf. He killed his father to protect me. To protect us."

Nikko squeezed my hand tight, his palm damp and shaking. "I was wrong to claim your daughter like I did. But I love her, and I want her to be happy. I released her from my claim, but she came back to me."

My dad's face didn't soften. "Do you believe this nonsense? I don't trust him, Luna. You shouldn't either."

"You don't know him like I do. All you know is what his father was like, but Nikko is nothing like that. He's good, and kind, and noble..." I took a deep breath and braced myself, "and I'm going to mate with him and join his pack."

Zander grimaced in disgust, and Dad held his chest like it was caving in. "Luna, no! How can you choose him over your own family?"

Guilt and fear that I was losing them threatened to bow my own body, but I resisted it. "It doesn't have to be a choice. He's offered a truce. He wants to end the feud between the packs. All you have to do is accept it."

"How can I trust him? His father spent the last 20 years looking for an opportunity to destroy me and our pack."

"And Nikko just risked everything to protect you!" I screeched, my body shaking with frustration. Nothing I could say would convince him to trust Nikko, and that meant I would have to lose one of them.

Amazingly, Nikko stayed calm, and he stroked a hand

down my back, trying to soothe me. "I understand why you don't trust me, Lupin. But trust your daughter. Believe in her. I do. So much so, I'm sharing the role of alpha with her. We're going to lead the pack together."

Dad's menacing scowl faltered. I jumped in, hoping to knock down more of his resistance. "Maybe someday the packs can come together again, as one. That's what I want to work towards. But it can't happen unless you agree to the truce."

He stared at me, his face twisted up with conflicting emotions, but said nothing.

I swallowed down my pain and moved towards the door. "I'm going inside to pack."

Nikko tried to follow me, but my brother blocked his path. "Don't even think about it."

I headed inside where the familiar scents of home threatened to overwhelm me. Forcing myself to stay strong, I grabbed a large suitcase and dragged it to my room then filled it with the treasures that meant the most to me, glad I had a chance to take them this time. They were mementos of a life that was gone forever. An innocence I could never regain. I filled the rest of the case with clothes, although I left a lot of them behind. My old jeans and ratty hoodies didn't seem appropriate for a newly mated alpha.

I was a different person now. I'd changed so much in the last few days. Matured from a cocky teen into a strong, powerful woman. I embraced the change, even though it scared me. All along, I'd believed I was meant for something greater than being a simple housewife like my parents expected of me, and I was right. This was what I was born for, to mend the rift between our packs and lead them into a better future. Hopefully my father would be able to see that eventually.

When my suitcase was full, I gave my old room one last look then headed back outside. My heart lifted when I saw my father seated on the top porch step, and Nikko on the bottom one. They both stood up when I came out.

My father turned towards me and held his arms out. I quickly abandoned my suitcase and went to him. "I don't want to lose you, Luna, and I'd like to see an end to this feud. I'm going to agree to the truce."

"Oh Dad!" I tightened my hold on him till he grunted like I was hurting him.

"You'll come back to see us sometime, won't you? You'll always be welcome here." He murmured into my hair.

"Of course, Dad. I'll come back so much you'll get sick of me. But…" I glanced at Nikko. Much of the tension had eased from his body, and he was smiling softly. "What about Nikko?"

Dad let go of me and walked down the steps. His face was stern, but he held out a hand. "I don't want to be enemies with my daughter's mate."

Nikko shook his hand, but my father clamped down and didn't let go of it. "But if you hurt her, I'll kill you."

"Dad!" I barged in between them.

Nikko flexed his hand after my father dropped it, but he didn't drop his grin. "I'll take care of her, sir."

I turned to look at Zander who was leaning against the porch column, arms across his chest. I gave him a strong look and nodded towards Nikko. Zander rolled his eyes and scowled but dropped his arms and headed down the steps.

"Friends?" Nikko stepped forward with his fist out.

Zander grudgingly bumped it with his own. "Let's start with not enemies."

Nikko chuckled. "Good enough for now."

I reached out and grabbed my brother in a bear hug. He didn't seem as big as he used to, but it was probably me who had changed. I felt stronger, more powerful, and confident now that everything would work out.

Nikko and I walked towards the truck, but I stopped at the door and turned back to my father. "You should tell Mom about all this. I think she could handle it. Girls are stronger than you think."

He smiled and nodded. "You certainly proved that, didn't you?"

I grinned and climbed in Nikko's truck. Then we headed back to tell our pack the war was over.

The End.

Liked this story? You'll love Dragon Scarred, book 2 in the Supernatural Sanctuary series.

Dear Reader,

If you enjoyed this book, will you please take just one more minute to write a review?

Reviews are critical to an author's success, plus they give us the warm fuzzies! It doesn't have to be long or glowing; just a few honest words and a star rating would be awesome!

Do you know someone who would like this book? Then let them know about it! You'll be helping a friend find their next great read and a new author they might enjoy.

Thanks so much for reading,
Kellie

Kellie McAllen is a USA Today bestselling author who has her nose in a book whenever she can. When she's not reading or writing, she also likes to guest judge on DWTS (from her living room), watch cat videos, and eat too much pizza and chocolate. She lives in North Carolina.

www.kelliemcallen.com
kellie@kelliemcallen.com

Printed in Great Britain
by Amazon